Coming from Nothing

Matthew McKeever

Winchester, UK
Washington, USA

First published by Zero Books, 2018
Zero Books is an imprint of John Hunt Publishing Ltd., Laurel House, Station Approach,
Alresford, Hants, SO24 9JH, UK
office1@jhpbooks.net
www.johnhuntpublishing.com
www.zero-books.net

For distributor details and how to order please visit the 'Ordering' section on our website.

ISBN: 978 1 78535 619 3
978 1 78535 620 9 (ebook)
Library of Congress Control Number: 2016961472

A CIP catalogue record for this book is available from the British Library.

Design: Stuart Davies

Printed and bound by CPI Group (UK) Ltd, Croydon, CR0 4YY, UK

What people are saying about

Coming from Nothing

A Nabakovian 'Old World meets New World' story, but instead of corruption meets innocence, it's pathos and degradation meets more pathos and degradation, as Carrie's and Jules's lives slowly unravel while they fail to bridge the gap between worlds. McKeever brings to the story a Martin Amis – like ability to find the moments of humanity, beauty, and redemption in characters struggling and failing (and failing to struggle) to lift themselves out of the muck and mire. *Coming from Nothing* is a literary beignet sweetened by a rich powdering of philosophical speculation. The metaphysics of gender, the nature of personal identity, the relations among mind, body, information, and society — all of these contribute to a central philosophical enigma. Are Carrie's and Jules's driftingly intersecting lives governed by the causal powers of absences, or by the absence of causal powers?

Josh Dever, Professor of Philosophy, University of Texas at Austin.

Coming from Nothing

Acknowledgments

I'd like to thank Poppy Mankowitz and Caitlín Nic Íomhair for lots of very generous and helpful feedback, and for encouragement. I'd also like to thank the Royal Institute of Philosophy for awarding me a Jacobsen Fellowship, during the tenure of which I wrote the first draft, and my PhD supervisor, Professor Herman Cappelen, who employed me during the writing of the second (and third and . . .) draft(s). Finally, I thank Zero Books, for taking a chance on me.

1

—Load of old fucking bollocks.

—That's . . . an opinion, I guess. So you're a, what, gender essentialist?

—Well, I don't know, but like.

He picked up the book beside him and started reading: 'The feminist appropriation of sexual difference whether in opposition to the phallogocentrism of Lacan blah blah. Blah. Blah. Blah.' Page 38. Like, what is that?

—What? You want it to be easy?

—Easier anyway.

—Well, dude, life ain't easy.

Said Carrie to Jules. She was wearing a green raincoat, the collar of which was popped up and threatened to engulf her head. Her eyes were cool and blue, but there was a sallowness to her complexion that reflected a bad night's sleep and, maybe, a lack of vitamin D. She spoke quickly with a southern American accent.

—It's just so . . . theoretical.

—Well, it's called 'theory' for a reas . . . actually wait!

She hit him on the arm.

—I guess for you it *is* a load of fucking bollocks because you're an essentialist, right? You locate it all in the bollocks or lack thereof.

—Well, firstly, it's 'bollocks' not 'ball-ox', and secondly I'm not an essentialist. I just want someone I can understand.

—Don't we all. . . . Well, whatever, it was a good joke right?

—I'll give you that, it was a good joke.

She smiled at him, then rubbed her blue jeans for no clear reason, as if she were wiping her hands off.

Jules was ruddy and short-haired and also wearing an engulfing jacket. His newly grown beard, a source of amusement and/or alarm to friends and/or family was not too impressive, but his face was symmetrical and she thought he was handsome. So she was happy, when she had asked him if she was in the right place for the tutorial (she had been unable to make her regular time this week), with his eager yes, guessing correctly he wanted to chat. And sitting down beside him she noticed gladly that he smelled good, or at least deodorized, which mitigated the fear of the unattractive beard.

They were outside a room on the fifth floor of Trinity College Dublin's arts block, sitting on a deep window ledge in front of wet glass, waiting for the tutorial for their class (Em)bodied selves, about feminist theories of literature.

—So you like this stuff, is it?

This was Jules, in a bland middle-class Dublin accent.

—Yeah man, for sure. It must be right.

—It must?

—Yeah, it must.

—That's a bold statement.

—Well, I mean . . . I don't wanna make this conversation *entirely* testicle-based, but what if someone cut a person's—let's say, your—balls off?

Jules laughed, but not very uncomfortably.

—No, no, I'm making a point. This isn't like some misandrist rant. Point is, that wouldn't make you no longer a man, right?

—No.

—And say you're paralysed completely—that doesn't make you no longer a person, right?

—No.

—So there! Your body doesn't define you, so you're an anti-essentialist.

—Hmm. I guess, like. It's just . . . why does it have to be so fancy? Why can't they just say that instead of all these words? Just less . . .

—Theoretical?

—Right. And like I mean . . . where is everybody?

Gesturing toward the empty hallway, he continued:

—What time is it? My phone's dead.

—Quarter after. Is this definitely the place?

—Been here last ten weeks, so yes. Did you check your email in the last couple of hours?

—Oh, no. Actually, I couldn't work out how to sync it to my phone.

—Can you just check in the browser?

She was doing. There was an awkward pause as it loaded, which Jules broke.

—I can show you how to sync, it's kind of awkward, I think they got the port wrong on the . . .

—Oh, cancelled! Uhh . . . oh, Deeurrmid, is that right?

—No, that's profoundly unright. 'Diarmuid'.

He said, laughing at her pronunciation, and causing her to laugh in turn.

—Well he's sick.

—Oh. No Butler for us then I guess. What a tragedy.

And then there was a pause. Jules looked down at his crossed legs, shy, uncertain. Carrie, more normal, asked:

—Do you want to get a coffee? We can, uh, have our own seminar, who needs Deeuhhh?

—'Diarmuid'. Sounds like a plan.

Carrie was in Dublin for six months visiting from Louisiana State University. There were no neat comparisons between the programs here and those in her home university, with the result that she took a wide range of courses: a first-year introduction to classical Greek literature, this third-year English course, a second-year metaphysics class and an independent study, also affiliated with the English department. While it was intellectually stimulating, the fact that she went from class to class—and, moreover, frequently joined classes among a cohort who all knew each other already—made it very difficult to make friends. Now, with Christmas approaching, and nearly half her time gone, she's started to get used to the dull ache that accompanies the empty weekends, where she'll generally go to some event alone or stay in her room in the halls, or simply walk around the city, it now more often than not raining and dulled with familiarity, heading over to the north side to the cheap supermarkets and second-hand bookshops, or getting lost around the leafy suburbs near the halls, the green of the leaves, almost overwhelming a few months ago, now gone from the streets.

Jules was also lonely, or at least somewhat alone. He had moved from being an incredibly introverted nerdy teen to being a mildly less so young adult. In the past year or so, he had come to realize that he might be desirable to the opposite sex, and was suffering something like Carrie: although he knew his classmates, when he started college he was so awkward that he never formed close bonds with them, and now that he wanted to it felt too late.

It was in an effort to overcome this that he was here. His degree was computer science, and he was just auditing this class. He claimed that it was because he was interested in feminist theory, truly enough, but the fact that he imagined it would be populated by women was not a small part of his decision. So far, though, his strategy of sitting quietly by himself in the corner had not been of much help in meeting people.

It's thus eagerly that they descended the stairs together, and after an hour or so awkwardness dispersed, and after two hours they were walking up the street for lunch, and after three they both realized something good was happening.

* * *

—And so, uh . . .

Earlier that morning, in the lecture they had unwittingly been sharing all semester, a nasally Californian, with big dark-rimmed glasses, a black suit over a white shirt, and a nose piercing glinting occasionally in the light thrown off from her laptop, was giving a lecture.

. . . this idea of performativity, it really helps . . .

Here she modulated into a digression, with a slightly different cadence, a half-smile, a sense that she was talking with, not at.

—When I was a student, my supervisor told me, it was like, it loosened the muscles that had gotten hardened, the sex/gender dichotomy that had become so engrained in the way people thought of these things, that it was very liberating for some people . . . and that's how I've always thought of it, as like a massage of our concept of woman, I guess . . .

—But so it really helps break down certain divisions, of the way we tend to have this *naturwissenschaftlich* conception of the body as opposed to—as we saw, what, a couple weeks ago—the *Geisteswissenschaften*, as opposed to culture, society, religion, art, the realm of the spirit, in Hegelian talk. And so those people who might want to say, yeah yeah *gender* is socially mediated, struck through with language; language-struck, but there's still the undeniable corpore*al*ity . . .

And she sort of sung the progression of the vowels, lifting off at the second 'o' and kind of losing the 'i' in the landing.

—The bodiness of the body that's just there, a facticity as Heidegger would say. For Judy . . .

Everyone noiselessly groaned at this first name, apart from the ones who smilingly thrilled. The division of the class into groaners and thrillers was exclusive and exhaustive.

—This evinces a certain failure of imagination. When she was writing, she was interested in things like drag, transgender people, camp. She thought that if you looked at the different ways in which femininity was expressed, you would see it needn't be tied to (what we call) female body parts. There's a spectrum, on which you could place the camp gay man at one end, the drag performer further along, and then transgender people who may have been born into male bodies but are women. Or vice versa, obviously.

So two aside points: first, biology bears this out: it would take us too far away to discuss, but you could look at stuff on intersex people (I think I put a link to a YouTube documentary on the handout). Second, it may be worth thinking about how technology changes the way we think of the body: how we often treat our smartphones as extensions of ourselves, et cetera. In this sense, I think the Butlerian framework has really proved prescient.

Uh, so yeah: not only is *gender* socially constructed, but to the extent we should even bother with the notion, there's no reason to think *sex* isn't either. And that's *anti-essentialism* about gender and sex.

This, from her experience, normally provokes more of a reaction. This was one of the first times she'd taught this material in Dublin, and she didn't know if it was the early hour, or herself, or the weird Irish reticence—so different from the US—to discuss things, but she looked out to a sea of apathetic slouched bodies.

But actually, if she had had superhuman eyesight, capable of taking in the faces of everyone in the room, she would have noticed two people, on completely opposite sides of the big room, both literally on the edge of their seats. These people were Jules and Carrie. Carrie, a thrilled smiler, was on the edge of her seat because she was fascinated. Jules was a noiseless groaner, and was on the edge of his seat because he really needed a piss.

—And, uh, well, I hope the strikingness of this thesis impresses you. And here I think Kant . . .

And she said this in the American way, still not used to the Anglophone European 'a' which makes the sage of Königsburg's name almost into the worst profanity.

—Is kinda relevant, because you can sort of view this as a

Kantian claim that the body is a *Ding-an-sich*, that it's inaccessible, indeed nothing shorn of the conceptual resources in which we, uh, clothe it: we make the body by what we say about it, just as for Kant we make the world spatio-temporal by applying our built-in concepts to it. And if people are interested in Butler's Kantianism . . .

And this was again, despite the fact she felt she wasn't being heeded, in the tone of talking to rather than at.

—Actually, I myself have a paper on that, and would be super happy to discuss it with you.

With better eyes, she would have noticed both Jules and Carrie scribble something at this point; Jules wrote illegibly and unhelpfully 'Kant paper', Carrie 'See Rosen(?) re B and Kant', the question mark taking the place where the date of publication should be cited, and 'Rosen' being the lecturer's name.

—But the point is, what's relevant for our immediate purposes? Well, I guess there are three things:

One, there's the pushing back against the sex/gender distinction. Two, there's the empirical stuff about drag, intersex, transgender people. And, like I include here our texts: so the approach to the body in Beckett's novels, the Shakespeare comedies with cross-dressing and misidentifications, and all that. Three, then there's the Kantian foundations.

And not all of this will be relevant, depending on which essay you choose. But at least the fluidity of the concept of body—the social construction of sex—will be relevant no matter what, and if you write on Butler in the exam you'll need to know it all.

And, uh, I guess that's about it for today. So discuss this with your tutors this week and any questions please email. And next week, as I said, we'll do the sort of opposing position, so try and read that Cisoux. I know it's not easy, but just give it a go and we'll talk about it next week.

Already at the start of the last sentence, there had been a rumble and the snap of myriad laptops being closed. Jules and

Carrie left with the rest of them, by separate exits, and were soon caught up in different dispersing crowds making the hubbub sound that most crowds, regardless of their sonic composition, end up making, and heading for the same place.

* * *

—So when did you realize that philanthropy was for you?

—Oh, well, I mean, isn't it for everybody?

Three days later, Jules and Carrie were lying together on her single bed in the halls in Dartry, she with her head on his chest, he with his lips on her forehead. It was coming up to 5pm, and already the sky through the window was dark blue, and people laden with shopping bags were shouting evening plans across the square.

Jules was working on micromicrotransactions. Microtransactions are small payments for small things; instead of subscribing to an online paper, you pay a small amount, say 25 cents, for each article you want to read. Similarly, you buy songs instead of albums, episodes instead of box sets, and so on.

Jules's thought was to go one level lower: to get people to sign up for his site 1010 (said 'one oh one oh'), and pledge to make a micromicrotransaction to a charity for every microtransaction one made. The suggested value was 10 percent, like a contemporary equivalent of tithing. The thought was that these transactions would be so small that people wouldn't notice or care, and so they'd find themselves doing good despite themselves, indeed constantly being tiny forces for good in the world.

—Yeah, but not everybody does anything about it. What made you do something about it?

—CS302, Computers and Society.

—Oh. So it's just for a grade?

—I mean, no, I really think it's good, if it would work, that it would work. I mean, that's obvious, right? That helping people is good . . . but it's like, maybe I don't like really feel it on a deep visceral level like I think you maybe do . . .

He had been impressed yesterday when, standing outside the arts block, Carrie had gone up to an old lady who looked lost and distressed and offered to help her, as others stood around gawping.

—But that's not bad. There's different ways you can help people. For me, it's like, I'm good at patching. Do you know what that is?

—Like . . . sewing?

—No, no . . . say you've got a piece of code that's meant to do something, and it doesn't work. Just doesn't work. You type it out exactly like in the textbook, say . . .

He started to get up.

—What are you doing?

—I just want to write it, show you a bit of pseudo-code.

—Please, in fact, *don't* show me a bit of pseudo-code. Continue to be my pillow.

—Okay, well, basically sometimes a program won't work, but you can play with it so it does, and it doesn't do it like it's meant to . . . wait, this is easier—say your chair has one too-short leg, and you put something under it to steady it. That's like patching it, getting it to perform its function in a different way, mending it, and like, the way I see it, this micromicrotransaction stuff is like a patch. Like humans should be good, but for whatever fucked-up reason they're aren't, so I patch 'em up, make 'em be good in a weird way, sort of like trick 'em by making being good psychologically unrecognisable . . . you think that's weird?

—Well . . . it's different. But I can see it, I guess. But, do you not think that it should come from within, that people should be good because they want to be?

—Nah. I mean how's that been working out so far in human history? If there were such things as forced labour camps where the labour was to be good, I'd be down with them.

—Wait, wait . . . what about this—if you could hypnotize one person to constantly do altruistic acts his whole life, would you?

—I don't know . . . see that's the thing with you philosophy types, it's always these silly cases. Point is, micromicro-transactions are nothing like that, they know what they're doing, no trickery.

—I get ya, I get ya.

— You sound unsure?

—Nah, nah, I get ya, Mr. Roboto, you're just trying to understand our human ways with the benefit of your pseudo-something.

And she moved her hand from his bicep to his stomach, and put her finger in his belly button, and he tittered. Happy to change the topic, he continued:

—I am, I am. Mr. Roboto, I like that. I might change my name by deed poll.

—Incidentally I been meaning to ask . . . 'Jules'? No offence but was your mom high when she named you? Is she like a royalist or something, like crown?

—Nah, the opposite.

—The opposite? What she's a republican?

—Yep, well, she's French. And it's actually 'Jules' as in Verne.

—Oh shit, listen to you! You speak French. You don't sound French. Or look French. Are you sure you're French?

—Je ne peux pas le nier.

—Oh shit, well I don't know what the fuck that means, it sounds pretty hot. . . . So it's not 'Jules', but everybody calls you 'Jules'. So everybody calls you the wrong thing? Well I'ma *zzhhule* you from now on.

—Please don't. . . . And anyway, 'Carrie', what's that, is that like short for Carantha?? What was your mum thinking?

—Eh, you're speaking ill of the dead, man.

—What?

—My mom's dead.

—Fuck, shit, oh . . .

— . . .

He was puzzled as to how that couldn't have come up already; thought, for one horrible moment, that it *had* come up last night in the pub and he'd forgot. In fact, Carrie had managed to successfully steer the conversation away from family any time it nearly came up, so successfully, in fact, that Jules hadn't realized. Now she had decided to steer the conversation toward family, feeling the time was right.

—It's okay. Like there's nothing to say. It's unambiguously bad.

—Uh, when did it happen?

—Like, final year of middle school?

—When's that? What age?

—Oh, like fourteen. It was . . . sudden.

—Jesus . . . well, I mean, I guess at least . . . did you . . .

She could tell he was winding up for some inane question or variation on how she was making her mother proud, variants of which always came out at about this time.

—Eh. Maybe don't say anything?

—Okay.

—Thanks, robo . . . man.

2

—You'll be tired when you get here, probably just want to sleep.

—I'll be tired?

He sent a jpg of Nic Cage's face with 'you don't say' printed beneath it.

—But nah, I bet I'll have energy being there and finaalllly seeing you. —Second wind.

—I hope you'll have plenty of wind for me . . . —lol that's not what I meant . . . —Energy, I hope you'll have energy.

—lol I will I'm sure. —Can't believe one sleep away and I'll be there.

It had been about eight months since Carrie left Dublin one very early April morning, in a farewell outside terminal two that had brought Jules, uncharacteristically, to tears.

Neither really knew what was going to happen: each had said, honestly, they wanted to see the other, but each suspected the other of being polite, or rather that their feelings would weaken with distance.

Their mutual confusion was soon more or less resolved. Having taken a bus back to O'Connell Street, the city now light and awake, Jules was making his way south when Carrie messaged him on whatsapp to say she'd checked in, beginning an eight-month conversation punctuated only when one or the other slept.

They shared everything about their lives, and their lives' daily ups and downs, in a way that somehow made them closer than when they were together: the imperative to keep the conversation going, and the lack of a mutually salient conversational topic (as provided by restaurants, films, etc., when they were together) meant each ransacked their day for items to convey: for funny things they saw on the Internet or in real life, for mild good news to share or mild bad news to be commiserated about, or advice about things which they could easily have worked out by themselves. They looked at the world with each other's eyes, and the world looked new.

And their sex life, or at least the passion that underlay it, didn't die either: they sent each other pictures and videos and developed the habit of skyping first thing Louisiana time, which for Carrie was around 11am, or 5pm for Jules, when she had just gotten out of the shower, and she would sometimes flash a boob to the camera, and he would show the effect the boob flashing had on him. They each also, but especially the more verbal Carrie, wrote stories either riffing on previous sexual encounters they had in the halls in Dartry, or in the place of their anticipated meetup in New Orleans, of which Jules had as good a sense as one can have of a place without ever being in it.

It was a miraculously peaceful time for them both: the uncertainty occasioned by Carrie's pending departure, which had always hung over them in Dublin, fled and was replaced with comfort. Although Jules's life was superficially similar to before: library, lectures, the odd quiet night out, it felt so much different, so much less alone. And Carrie, who had been trying to flee Louisiana her whole life, came to see it with new eyes: through Jules's. She found herself thinking of her state with a view to what would be interesting to him in it, and this borrowed perspective helped to minimize her own which had been so oppressive.

Soon he was making concrete plans to actually be there. The summer wasn't so good for Carrie, and then come September both would be back at university, and so he started looking at flights to arrive for a period before the start of the term in the new year, and around September, completely confident about buying non-refundable tickets months in advance, he booked ten days in early January.

* * *

It felt like something looming out of the darkness, an island spatiotemporally separated. Jules could smell garbage, cigarettes, and heat, hear the sounds of mixed American accents blurring together; Carrie's nose and ears were dulled through familiarity.

They were walking around one of the streets off Bourbon, holding hands, having just come from a bar where old couples were smoking and drinking and dancing by the counter to a band which was regularly asking for tips.

The sky above was a purpley sort of thing, but the day's heat and Carrie's warm hand in his, and the beer, and the incipient jetlag, elevated it to something entirely new for Jules, and he kept on looking up, as they threaded their way from street to street, confused by its newness, by this new style of balconied housing for which he lacked words, and by happiness.

It had seemed so effortless he didn't understand. There was the before life, well-represented by greyness, rain on the Liffey, the lower floor of the library and slow nights in Doyle's, and now this: all senses delirious, a hand warm in his, a glow in the belly. He turned her around and kissed her on the street, something the doughty Irish him wouldn't gladly do, and his barely functioning mind almost forgot himself in the warm of her mouth until she broke it off and smiling shiny lips filled his eyes.

They wandered round the French quarter for a while and then went and got beignets, sitting drunk and sweating on the terrace of a cafe at a tiny table, surrounded on all sides with chatter, their lips dusty with sugar and their pipes occasionally jerkily expectorating it. Conversation, which had flown so effortlessly since she had come to meet him at the airport, kind of stalled, and they found themselves looking into each other, wordless, for a while, and when they started next to converse, he found that he couldn't remember a thing. He had fallen temporarily amnesiac and thought he was lost in Dublin, but she was somehow back in Dublin, which had suddenly jumped to summer, and thereafter things were blank for a bit.

He woke, or memory returned, in darkness and a fan whooshing overhead, Carrie on top of him, fucking him. He touched her body, forced her hips into his, and then shifted and lifted her up and repositioned her in front of him, and was just shifting his weight over, his left hand firmly on her hip, when he fell off the bed, and tangled up with him she fell too, and her bum and lower back hit him square in the face.

Then lights came on and there was the taste of iron and his tongue noticed something missing and his nose was broken and at least one tooth was lost. He didn't really register what had happened, or appreciate its significance, and so when horrified Carrie, whose lack of sleep deprivation and knowledge of the American medical system made her realize that some hellish hours were ahead, bent down over him with a quickly found towel, he thought she was trying to sit back down on him and directed her, reaching up and grabbing her hips.

—What the fuck are you doing?

—C'mon.

—You're hurt. We need to go to the emergency room like *now.*

—Ah, it can wait, c'mon.

—You look like a fucking zombie! Get up. You're hurt. Is it painful?

—Nah, it's grand. We can go in the morning.

—You might have a concussion, and you definitely need a dentist ASAP.

—It's fine.

And he closed his eyes, as if to sleep, smiling happily a gappy bloody smile. Carrie looked over him, naked and horrified.

They went to the emergency room, he gradually threading the thoughts together that this is not a good situation, and the pain now coming in full force, combining with the massive dehydration caused by first the flight, and then the beers and walking about in the heat. His head, both in and out, burned with pain. And his stomach was now roiled with upset and anxiety.

So he spent his first night with Carrie, his head on her lap, in the waiting room, pained from four or five different sources. They waited for five hours before he got good drugs and stitches to his lip, and they removed the shards of teeth, about which there is nothing to do while here (not that he could or would pay for it), and sent him home.

The day breaking, they returned to the room it all started in, the clothes they wore downtown discarded across the floor, each mentally and physically drained, and went to bed. Carrie slept for three hours, fitfully and unhappy, and he slept for fifteen hours, the whole of the second day of his nine-day (excluding days lost to travel) trip.

The remaining days were not spent pleasantly. Jules came round to the land of the living the next day, and felt ready to take on day three of the intricately planned itinerary Carrie had joyfully made for them, and shared with him, in the weeks before their trip.

There was tension from the start. While he had been resting, Carrie had been feeling that time was slipping away from them. Although she didn't blame him for the accident, and threw herself into the creation of chicken-noodle soup and the provision of ice chips, she was itching with disappointment. Like, realistically, when would they have a chance to do this again? She couldn't stop thinking about the future, about the time he was wasting in bed, and this drove her crazy. Jules, for his part, was too buried under fatigue and opioids and the fact that he would now have to find, conservatively speaking, a few thousand euro for medical treatment to be particularly heedful of how she must feel, and indeed treated her with a sort of entitlement, actively getting annoyed when she failed to turn the microwave off defrost and thus delayed a meal of his by seven minutes. So, they both couldn't blame each other, but each did, and all the time the clock was ticking.

That day, nevertheless, they went to one of New Orleans's most famous tourist attractions, the St. Louis Cemetery. They had talked a lot on Skype about this, and were particularly looking forward to Nic Cage's douchebag pyramid mausoleum. This had led, in the last couple of weeks, to a lot of their communication being in the form of sending one another Nic Cage memes, which, remarkably, are numerous enough to handle most conversational situations.

And duly they did see it, along with the rest of the vaults. But the atmosphere was sombre: Jules was quiet on account of some residual tenderness (his muscles, leg muscles especially, seemed drained of strength, despite the bed rest), and his quiet made Carrie anxious, and when she asked him if he was quiet because he was feeling bad, and he quietly said a wee bit but tried to smile it off, Carrie became quiet and started to feel bad. And as soon as they had finished the tour, after which they had planned to see some of the cool old timey houses in the area, she asked if he wanted to just go back to the house, and, thinking that's what she wanted—because she was so quiet—he said yes, and back they went. And Nic Cage was never mentioned again.

The next day seemed to start well. They woke at roughly the same time and spent the morning huddled up together under the blankets, finally just talking normally, without the eager tension of the first day or the gnathological minutiae of the next ones, making a plan for the day that both could be excited about: lunch, then seeing some sights. And that happy mood led naturally to one thing, and another thing, and was going to lead to sex—but then, despite Jules's having been bombarded with feverish erotic pain dreams, then it didn't, it fizzled out suddenly and conclusively. This didn't exactly help the atmosphere, and the day was spent awkwardly lounging around the apartment.

Day five was lost entirely. Pretending a flare-up of the receding pain, Jules stayed in bed all day, sweating and staring at the ceiling, sad. Carrie, going along with the ruse, spent an inordinate amount of time—the whole afternoon, more or less—getting groceries, feeling welling up in her, in a big Walmart, tears that nevertheless wouldn't come, driven crazy by the time that was being lost, as he lay there, at the distance that had somehow come between them, ruing this whole trip, or at least the accident which had started things.

Things continued, in a confusing way. Neither knew where they stood, or what really was happening. Each thought the other didn't want them there, but each was receptive to evidence that they did, and so a morning that started with a friendly 'good morning' led (on two occasions) to close days, where they finally did get to see a bit of the town, and it felt like the trip was going well. But on two other occasions, through a lack of sleep or melancholy or whatever, if the day started less well, it continued so. When it came time for him to leave, the ride to the airport was dull and quiet, neither experiencing the rising sobs that had eventually got out when they took the bus to Dublin Airport eight months ago. Both were paradoxically upset, and disheartened by their lack of upset, by the mess that lay behind them, by the utter failure of what they'd waited so long for. At the airport they hugged and Carrie kissed his purpley blue cheek and then his lips, and told him to tell her when he arrived safely, and he did, but that was that, until Jules texted her a year later.

3

—Fuck off u dumb, probably fat, whore.

Nine or so months later, Carrie was on a date.

—Ha, look at that? See it's the epistemic humility I appreciate there, the way he—quite rightly—hedges on my being fat. Coz you see, dumb and whore though I may be, fat I most certainly am not.

—People like that . . .

Charles shook his head mournfully. That seemed to mark the end of his contribution; Carrie sighed. But he continued:

—Who said that?

—This bus ain't gonna be here for fucking . . . I'll pop into the store, get a beer. Want anything?

This last as she was already walking away. She was sure he wouldn't want something, or if he did, it would be toothpaste or drain cleaner or whatever it is unspeakably dull people buy on hot Saturday nights in New Orleans.

They were on Chartres Street, waiting for a bus to take them uptown, where they both lived within a couple blocks of each other. It was that that had made her swipe right. Well, that and he was inordinately good looking: he looked like what you might expect a Scandinavian world-champion swimmer would look like, albeit with a softness to his eyes.

But it was at least 50 percent because of where he lived. She had been under the impression that her area was populated entirely by people three or four times her age, and had thought that even if the date turned out bad, there was at least a reasonable chance he might have similarly aged roommates whom she could befriend.

This had been an issue. Most of her friends had left the city after graduation in June. And although she had just started grad school in September she was doing it part-time and online, for financial reasons (the university had offered a series of decent scholarships in the hope of making the online program be seen as more respectable and as a viable alternative to full-time study).

A consequence of this, though, was that she didn't have office space on campus, and so far her attempts to make contact with the few full-time English grad students in the department had been mixed, and so she needed to make friends.

But alas Charlie—she should have known that his name was a bad omen, redolent of home in Lake Charles—was no good. He lived alone, also in an apartment block full of old people. Unlike her, though, this didn't seem to bother him. Indeed, an off-hand joke she made about the stench of death in the hallways provoked from him the stern furrowed brow that in the few hours she had known him she had come to despise.

The whole thing had started off badly. Attempting to appear assertive, he'd decided to direct the evening, and had taken them to a bar which was both packed with tourists and already playing music. This made conversation next to impossible, with the result that the first half hour or so of their meeting was filled with either silence or 'WHAT?'s.

Then, once they'd managed to get out, and go to a quieter place at *her* suggestion, they had had a weird conversation about anxiety disorders. Carrie was feeling a combination of awkward and tipsy at this point, and this made her blab, and for some reason she shared that she'd been dealing with some anxiety stuff recently. His response was to start talking about *his* anxiety. Perhaps this came about through an attempt to establish some common ground, but if it were so, it misfired. While she had quickly realized that psychological problems are not first-date fodder, he didn't, and spent what was realistically perhaps only five minutes but felt like an eternity detailing the severity, longevity, symptoms (most disturbingly, he couldn't eat in restaurants without having a couple of drinks beforehand, which made Carrie feel genuinely sorry for him), and even putative etiology of his troubles. Carrie felt herself longing to be back in the noisy bar, wondering how someone so good looking had managed never to be properly socialized.

In the store, filled with souvenir tat and T-shirts with profanities, she felt some release, both to be away from him and to be in air-con. She was wearing a short summery dress revealing a large portion of her upper torso, which was tan and had a sheen of sweat. A little bit of acne scars showed through slightly inadequately applied foundation which she hadn't bothered touching up after her first bathroom break. She went to the fridge and looked for a beer. Charlie liked beer, and was serious about it, so she was set on getting the worst possible beer she could find, consistent with her not hating it, and settled on 24-oz cans of Bud Light. She got two, one for home. After all, it was only, oh it was 11 already. It felt much earlier, but she didn't conclude from that that she had had a better time, but that her brain couldn't get her head around Charlie in the evening. She imagined him noctivating at 6:30pm every night, just as work ends and people can unwind, retreating from fun.

That it was already 11 made her think of how many drinks she'd had, and now she totted it up she was a bit tipsy. She came out and the heat hit her again, and before her on the sidewalk was a group of dude-bros walking in single file separate from one another, communicating by calling back or shouting forward, all dressed in white and with southern accents even she thought rustic. She sat back on the ledge and Charlie told her he'd googled that the bus was in ten minutes, and so she earnestly set to drinking essentially the capacity of her stomach in that time.

—Who was that guy?

Carrie stopped, confused. He continued:

—The rude one?

She was confident, for some unclear reason, that he meant the middle white-shirted guy, who had, indeed, been saying something rude.

—I don't know, you know as much as me.

—But he was messaging you?

The time it took her to draw the dots told her she'd better be careful with the beer. She made to light a cigarette to clear her head.

—Oh, just some troll.

Thinking it might lead to *some* sort of interesting conversation, she took out her phone. She didn't really need to, but she tapped through to the guy's Twitter page.

—Alt-right. Problematic. Patriotic. Trad. Hashtag feminisismiscancer.

She tried to say the last block as it was written, joining the words into each other, and laughed and gulped her beer.

—Horrible.

With his furrowed brow.

—Eh, that's life.

—Does it happen often?

—Yeah, pretty often. I want to, they don't let me interact with them, I'd love to play with them then mute them but that's unprofessional they think. It's annoying. So I have to just block and go on.

—What provoked it?

—Oh, good question . . . it was ahhhh it was actually a piece by me. That's hilarious. It was this academic thing, the thing I was saying, the feminist body stuff. Oh man, there's no way he read that. I wish I wouldn't have already blocked him, love to know what he thinks about *Gender Trouble*.

One of the positive steps Carrie had made toward getting a group of friends was joining the LSU FemSoc, taking over the social media account and occasionally posting short primers on relevant issues in feminist theory which were meant to be accessible to people without the background.

—Alt-right, what is that?

—It's like, I don't know, I think it's just another name for racist really. Like Trump supporters. 'Alt-right' is meant to sound trendy or some shit.

With a disconcerting metal screech, the bus rounded the corner, and Carrie, with not a huge amount of dignity, stood by a trash can downing her beer. They then rode the bus. She, full of stomach, got off suddenly at the stop before hers, so that there was no chance for a final goodbye and potential 'well we should do this again sometime', calling 'it was nice to meet you' behind her as she hopped happily off the bus.

Her premature exit meant she had to walk across some wasteland to get home. She opened the second beer. Crickets chirped somewhere in the dark of hedges or behind the single-story wooden houses, and she could smell her own sweat on the straps of her top as she bent over her phone, simultaneously reading the Internet and using the light to guide her across the land.

* * *

Sometimes, Carrie remembers things weirdly. The night of her mother's death, for example, in her head begins with an image of her family house, like an establishing shot.

The night it happened she was first in her bedroom, and then in her bed, asleep, so she knows it's a false memory. And because that's the very *first* image creeps her out and makes her cast doubt on the rest.

But some, she knows, must be true. The memory continues without action, more of a feeling tone. It's not the first feeling she had as she returned to consciousness that night. The first feeling she had was confusion; she heard a strange crying sound and noticed light coming from beneath the door, and her body knew, as bodies tend to know, it was sometime deep in the night, and that her mom, the only other person in the house, would have been long asleep. In the confusion of sleep, she thought it was an animal: a big feral cat, maybe, and once she'd got that in her head she was frightened of getting scratched. But that's not the feeling tone that comes next in her memory. The feeling tone is of terror.

She doesn't know what to make of the feeling. She thinks she probably didn't feel it until near morning. Things were for a long time a blur of new and strange sensations which she couldn't conceptualize. But she knows she started feeling it, and she never stopped feeling it, so it's consistent that the feeling is not part of the memory but something she is adding to it right now, for example, as she passes by the wasteland and gets on the head lit residential street a block from her apartment.

So that's not great, two of two false memories. And then the third—? The third is her mother's face all wrinkled up in a grimace that still makes her legs go a little weak and blood rush to her cheeks. It's a wrinkledness, she thinks, expressing a pain she can't comprehend, and for some reason what it most reminds her of is an animal's pain, of a ferocity she can literally not understand. She sees the face in her mind, but she wonders, is it really real? Did she see the face?

But she thinks maybe it is real, and she's quite confident that the memory of her getting up, scared but not a fraction of how scared she was about to be, is real. Then, unlike now, the night was slept through, and she didn't know what to do, what the procedure for night waking was. Now she turns on the bedside lamp, but she was younger then, and she didn't need a bedside lamp, so she groped in the dark to the door and opened it and there was her mom on the floor.

Then things passed very quickly. An ambulance came and it was windy and dark—she'd only been out so dark a handful of times before—and then she doesn't know if she fell asleep or what but she was at her grandparents' house. Then the sun rose, but not at all like the sun normally rises, all at once to be there when she's woken, but gradually throughout the night. And her grandfather was there, but hunched over and in pajamas and tearful and thus not in any way whatsoever like her grandfather. And then she was told her mother was dead.

And from that morning on her life was entirely different: she lived in a different house, among different people, in a world where the sun rises slowly and sometimes you're woken up surprisingly and a body suddenly ceases.

* * *

Carrie approached the apartment. Up ahead was a busy road, and she saw shining a McDonald's sign and a 7-Eleven, and the light did something to chase away her memories. She had lived in this place for two years, and, apart from the geriatric neighbours, there was one very annoying thing—her roommate Jordan. He was a strange combination of humourless and earnest and also pedantically right on. He was studying hospital management, and didn't really have much to talk about beyond hospital management.

And despite his involvement in the LGBT society (it was him, in fact, who had put the thought of FemSoc into her mind), she has never once seen him with a boyfriend. He seemed perfectly content to spend his Friday nights in watching TV (watching her TV, in fact) and sometimes he'd go to a coffee shop on Saturday afternoon with his friend Max, but she was very sure they were not fucking and she knew she shouldn't say or think this but really, she thought gays were more fun. She knows that probably it's just he's young and shy (he's four years younger than her) and probably still learning to be a man, but for some reason it irrationally annoyed her.

When she came back, at 11:20pm, now ready for bed, she saw Leslie Knope on the screen and smelled the popcorn he had microwaved for himself.

—Hiiiiiii. So, good date?

—Eh.

—Oh, no! That doesn't sound good!

—Yeah, this dude, well I'm pretty confident I won't . . .

Her phone buzzed.

—Be seeing him again, let's put it that way.

And she checks her phone and, oh, it's him.

—Or . . .

—Him?

—Yeah. He obviously had a different experience. Wants to see me again.

And her head is hidden behind the white door of the fridge she's looking in, but there's a long low

—Noooooooooooo

That ends in an

—Ah.

Which marks that's she's found a snack pack of crackers, chicken salad, and apple, unopened and which she'd been saving for the next time she'd got drunk.

—I'm sorry your date went badly.

—Eh, it's whatever. We played a game of, uh, anxiety-disorder uponemanship.

—Uh?

—Gingwhosmranggus.

Chicken salad hampering her articulation.

—Sorry, doesn't matter, it was fine.

Once she'd swallowed, to his puzzled look, she scrunched her face up in a what-a-kooky-world sort of look.

—These things happen, it was okay. How are you?

—Yeah, good thanks, big test on Monday.

—You always have test. . . . I'm glad I'm a PhD student, we don't gotta do *fuck all*.

It was a spondaic 'fuck all'.

—Hey, now . . . I read your new piece. I think even I could

follow it. Did you see salome.com retweeted?

Salome.com was a pretty well-followed, mainly satirical, feminist website.

—Oh, really? Wow. I guess that explains all the hate messages the FemSoc's been getting. I've really made it, two guys called me a cunt today, and one hypothesized that I was fat.

Jordan looked at her with mild disappointment for having said 'cunt', and she continued:

—Ah well, haters will hate. Nothing to get worked up about.

She took her half can of beer into her bedroom and drank it quickly, checking with pleasure the likes and retweets her article got. This and the beer made the night end much better than it had started, and she went to sleep happy.

4

A myoclonic jerk woke Carrie too quickly from nauseating dreams. She found her head off the pillow, an almost certainly wet sun against the window already, the air conditioner on too low for her dehydration-hot cheeks.

Her head hurt a bit and she felt her muscles weak and saw she had neglected to bring a glass of water to bed. This she makes to remedy, hopping up, in short shorts and a top, heading to the kitchen and drinking from a plastic cup with FRANK'S CREOLE written in faded letters and a faded painting of what may have been an alligator.

It's only 8am, but she knows she has no energy to do what she would normally do, go to the gym, then maybe shop, and then maybe write the blogpost she's been putting off. She thinks back to Charlie and the would-be troll and she loads up the troll's page and spends some time reading his tweets and those of his followers. She thought it would be funny: she remembered it amusing her last night. But it wasn't so fun. It was just constant idiotic racist abuse, and after a few minutes doing so, with a coffee inside her, she stopped, lying horizontal on the couch looking at the swinging fan above the light, her stomach tight with the caffeine-cum-alcohol panic. The world seemed a dark grey place, with these people out there spreading their uncontrollable thoughtless hate. Then she came across a tweet:

—Snowflakes are muslI'Ms i'm a muslI'MNOT! #tcot

Once she'd parsed it, she burst out laughing, and thought of variations on the theme. In general, she thought, so many of the tweets were so painfully stupid it would be doing someone a service to mock them. But she couldn't do that from the FemSoc account. She thought about creating a separate account to do so, but then had a better idea: she would make her own account *pretending* to be one of those people, try to build a following, and then eventually reveal it as a hoax.

This she did, calling herself @rightadjacent, a handle playing on a joke that had been going round whereby some mixed-race liberal had called themselves 'white adjacent' and had castigated themselves for the privilege they thereby inherited, and had been widely mocked. She used as her avatar a photo of an extreme close-up of her eye and the surrounding skin, thinking it had suitable Aryan *bona fides* as well as being impossible to trace to her.

Having set it up, she followed a bunch of alt-right accounts, included a link to breitbart.com in her bio, and sent her first tweet.

—Is #Shillary going to keep Nobrainer's plan to institute Shariah here? Lock up your wives, literally.

She laughed at this, especially the non-sequitur final sentence, but as she saw the refollows and then retweets come in, she started to feel a bit depressed and unamused again, and the hangover was waning a bit, so she decided to shake herself off the couch and shower and try to make something of the day.

Now that the date was out of the way, she was back to square one, friends-wise, and the prospect of weekends stretching out like this, with nothing planned and time bulging, made her uneasy. So she went to the supermarket to count the micromorts.

A micromort is a means of measuring activities in terms of increase in the chance of death they cause: one micromort is a one in a million chance of dying next year. So, 500ml of wine and 1.4 cigarettes are each one micromort (closely related is the concept of a microlife, which is half an hour of life expectancy: smoking a packet of cigarettes takes away nine microlives, a six pack of beer three, and so on).

Since hearing about it, Carrie had been periodically very taken with the idea. She liked to think of space peppered here and there with these little deaths: it seemed to imbue day-to-day life with, if in a blanched sense, the significance and meaning that attention to death does. And she took something akin to pleasure in totting up her own micromorts, as it seemed to provide sense to her often senseless days.

She was counting them now, peeking into others' baskets and balancing her own so as not to overdo it on the death. The others, though. Little deaths clamour in the wide cool isles. Twenty-four packs of red coke, frozen pizzas, microwavable burgers, ice cream, bacon, beer. Her shopping cart is comparatively lifeful. Not too much of a person for junk food, the eighteen pack of beer which she'll get started on later but will last a week and the chicken and what passes for French bread and potato salad that'll she graze on for dinner is side by side with kale and brown rice and muesli, produce and canned tomatoes and healthy food, enough for a week.

She gets home at around four and unpacks. Time stands still for a while and she eats some chicken and bread over the tabletop counter, checking the interactions on her FemSoc account. She thinks maybe she ought to do some reading for her online seminar on Wednesday but also thinks maybe the day's too long in the tooth, and what would instead be nice would be to sit on the balcony and drink beer and read some.

So that's what she does, and as the alcohol loosens her hungover muscles and joints, and she starts to feel mentally and physically lighter than she did, she feels a bit whimsical and decides to check in on @rightadjacent. She's got seventeen new followers and four people liked her ridiculous tweet. She reads the bios, laughing at them before following them back, seeing and hearing families occasionally pull into the complex, coming from the Walmart she was at, in shorts and T-shirts and summer tops, from hot cars into the hot parking lot.

Her attention was drawn again and again from her book—a thick theory anthology—to Twitter. There was something about it. The brutality of these people, who want to deport Mexicans, or protest outside abortion clinics, or ban Medicare, and make

Islam illegal. Such brutality is normally locked away because to act on it would involve doing something big and bad. But not here: these people could act on it in small or distant ways, by posting mean things, racist memes, by anonymously threatening to rape people they didn't like, and so on. Just as Carrie was fascinated by the micromorts in the aisles of Walmart, so she was fascinated by these tiny, almost unnoticeable movements toward the very, very bad, that penetrate into the fabric of life and spot it deep in the wool.

It gave her hope, the hope that the world was intelligible. For too long it had not been. She couldn't understand how unspeakable violence could just be there, in the day to day, ready to pop up. But now maybe she understood: it was just the tendency of life, or at least of a lot of life, to go that way. A sort of principal of destructive inertia: that a body, unless acted upon by an anti-destructive force, will continue toward its own destruction. The glare of others functions as an anti-destructive force, but the anonymity of the Internet checks it, and the natural destructiveness is manifest.

But maybe it wasn't intelligibility: maybe it was community. That people shared these urges for micro-destruction, these little quiet urges that are more or less completely ignorable, except maybe when you're hungover, or stand on the scales, or again when you read, say, how someone was doxed and forced to leave their home. Urges you can give into in the depths of the long weekend, or in the phone hidden in your pocket, where no one sees you. She found herself completely unsurprised that the possibility for anonymous Internet communication led to this, that anonymity breeds destruction.

It didn't feel like hope or intelligibility or community, though, sitting on the balcony a bit fuzzy already, the sun pushing itself onto her lowered eyes. But that was what kept her scrolling.

* * *

—It's machines dude, machines all the way up. You see, do you know Hobbes? Well Hobbes y'see thought that the whole world was mechanically organized, that . . .

—Wait, wasn't he the nasty brutish yada yada guy?

—He was! But he's more than that. Like, basically he thought we could make a science of everything in terms of the prevailing science of the time, which was, well I won't talk about it too much. But like, a billiard ball on a table was a machine, and a human was a machine, and the society in which that human found himself was a machine: mechanism. We're just like machines pushed and pulled here and there. My drinking this . . .

She drank some of her drink, and looked out onto the bright street.

—My wanting to drink this, my being here when I should be reading, all machines.

—That's wild.

Her interlocutor opined, and his wife moved her face in the direction of an agreeable smile. Carrie got the sense they didn't *really* think it was wild. He continued:

—It's like, uh, Schrödinger's cat.

—What is?

—Uh, I mean, could you say that we're not machines, we're just like, neither machines nor particles.

Carrie reflected that the problem with non-monologues, pleasant as they can be, was the non-monous nature of them. She was sitting in a bar the following Friday. It was late afternoon. A couple of gregarious out-of-towners had asked her where's good to eat, and the conversation had just sort of unfolded.

—Yeah.

Carrie said uncertainly, tipsy enough to not be polite enough to make something intelligible of what he said, tipsy enough also to want to tell her Really Cool Ideas to a worthless interlocutor.

—But you see what's cool is the idea that he got his whole sort of bag of concepts from the prevailing scientific and economic context. He saw us as machines because of when he lived, right? And you even get this before, like if you consider ideas that people were like horses in Plato and something kinda similar in early Buddhist stuff. Obviously, horses were very economically important back in the day, obviously.

—People were like horses? Hear that, horses.

This to his wife, whose interest in the conversation was quickly waning, and who was watching the passing show outside the bar with interest.

—So then, this is 'my philosophy' . . .

They had asked her what her philosophy was when she said she studied philosophy and literature. They perhaps hadn't expected her reply. Their philosophy was treat people well which, while nice, isn't exactly Aristotle.

—That personal identity is culturally relative, and our personal identity concepts are determined by guiding economic, social, and technological ideas of our culture.

—Awesome, like paradigm shifts? Philosophy of science?

—Yeah, like that.

Giving up the ghost of conversation.

—Oh! Y'all gotta go to the Carousel!

Although she had just started grad school, Carrie knew exactly what she wanted to do, and spent her time, sometimes to the detriment of her grades, doing it. There was a compulsory class on Milton which for next week's class she needed to read *Lycidas* and connect it to English pastoral, which is so screamingly tedious that, although she really, really tried this week, she managed one lead-headed read through before returning to her close reading of Locke's *Essay Concerning Human Understanding*, which itself has a sort of Hobbesian mechanism to it.

Even with that, today, she struggled, finding herself skipping dozens of pages at a time (she had previously read the abridged version and found it almost captivating; she regretted the scholarly propriety which made her go to the full-length one), and when it came to be four she felt she'd put in enough effort and so went into town for a change of pace and found herself hungry and thirsty, and hoping somehow to make something out of the ghost of a week that had been.

* * *

The crickets are maddening, omnidirectional and thus somehow adirectional: with movement, their chirrup neither retreats nor advances, Carrie is stuck in a world of cricket sound.

There's a little grassed-over, dried-out bayou by the path she walks home, replaying in her mind the conversations she had and re-reacting to them, her face now smiling, now pretending shock, now mouthing words she said or would have said.

The disappointment that it was that sort of people she always meets in bars, the weirdos and the finite, makes her long for a community. And that longing, and these crickets, cause her mind to turn to her grandma and grandpa's house, and to invisibility. Invisible is what she's always felt since her mom died. And it was weird, very weird, to go from visible to invisible. Her mom was sharp and keenly perceptive. If there were something wrong, she would know it instantly, sometimes even before Carrie herself did. Her grandparents were not sharp. She quickly realized she could get away with most anything, and to be in her room, while they were in their living room, was to be beyond the reach of their hearing and (practically) their locomotion.

That's by no means to say that they neglected her. It's just if they chose not to neglect her, she could hear them coming: could hear the beginning clumps of the walkers at the bottom of the stairs, or hear the click of the bedside light and rough stomps when one of them got up to piss after dark. And she then had as much time as she needed to close windows or turn down music or hide evidence.

At first, the invisibility was oppressive. It was just

fundamentally weird, she thought, that, for example, when a lamp fell and shattered no one came to see what had happened. That wasn't how it had been before. But soon, she came to revel in the freedom invisibility conferred.

What she most liked to do was leave: to go out via her window onto the garage roof and then shimmy down off it, and go out into the thick unkempt fields behind her house. At first she did this at study time, for brief periods, as a sort of dare with herself: would she get away with it? Would they, by chance, happen to come up and find her? Later she would do it in the dead of night, and then, there would be the same omnipresence of crickets, and she would feel the night air deep in her lungs and the complete darkness broken only, if at all, by her phone. She liked it so much, this big secret she had, this secret life only she knew of pure dark and crickets. She made of her isolation a feature, not a bug.

And once she realized this, and as she grew older, her secret life expanded. She could listen to music with swear words loudly or later watch porn, or eat candy or later drink vodka, or stay up as long as she wanted talking to her friends or later have boys shimmy up the same pipe she shimmied down. She was free. And that freedom never really left her, that sense that her life was one separated out, for herself only, that she could do whatever the fuck she wants because no one will tell her not to.

5

A microapocalypse, let's say, is something which increases the chances of an apocalypse by a small percentage. Voting for a climate-change sceptic, for example, depending on what you're voting for, is several microapocalypes. Carrie started committing microapocalypses.

It was so just fucking easy. A couple of weekends before Thanksgiving she was drunk at home, bored. It was the end of an entirely empty bored week, and she had no plans. So she thought she'd log in to her @rightadjacent account. The other day a somewhat liberal politician/lawyer had appeared on a new sketch show, and loads of people, including friends of hers, had been sharing it, saying how funny it was. This judge was being touted as a replacement of someone on the Supreme Court who had unexpectedly died and, though she was better than the alternatives, nevertheless she was known for being extremely hawkish on foreign policy. Of course, the right-wing friends of @rightadjacent didn't want this liberal replacement and had sought to try and make it seem politically unpalatable by kicking up a stink, spreading information and misinformation and straight-up insults.

When Carrie, scrolling through the destructive nonsense, noticed a tweet that contained a particularly relevant damning piece of information about the politician's views on foreign policy, she retweeted it, even though she knew, in so doing, she might, admittedly in a laughably small way, contribute to the Republican rival's getting favoured, and even though she knew that would be bad for the US and the world.

This she could kind of justify to herself: after all, the truth will out, right? But it didn't stop there. The politician in question had a history of some decisions that looked, from a distance, very problematic: in particular, she had made some rulings about black people that could be seen as racist. They weren't really, once you knew the full details of the case, as Carrie did, but they certainly looked so. Carrie spread the misinformation about the case, indeed helped to disseminate it in a more rhetorically effective manner, and doing so found herself retweeted a lot by eagle avatars and with a bunch of new followers.

Soon she had given up even the pretence that she was informing. The politician was rumoured to be a lesbian. As such, among her followers, she was the subject of a bunch of homophobic abuse. Carrie joined in, retweeting cruel or offensive comments about her looks, about her being manly, about her not being a trustworthy American woman. She knew, now, she had no justification, that what she was doing was bad, but if anything that just made it more appealing.

She didn't know why she was doing it. Partly it just seemed unreal: the link between cause and effect, between her typing things and things happening in the world, seemed so tenuous that she couldn't believe what she was doing would have any effect. And she hid it away, made it invisible to her day-to-day life: typically she would only go to it, like a guilty secret, when she had been drinking, and when she had finished, she would log out and not return to the site for days, not thinking at all about this dark side as she went about her daytime business. In that way she could easily cordon it off, and think of it as not belonging to her.

It was so small it almost felt like nothing, just a little nudge toward disaster, something as easily forgettable as Saturday's hangover is on Sunday. But it was large enough to feel like something, and Carrie liked it, she liked anonymously piloting the world slightly toward oblivion.

* * *

Jordan was crying and the room smelled of a roast dinner. It was

Thanksgiving. There had been tension in the apartment leading up to today: Carrie had felt it, trying to quell her irritation as he asked her again and again to confirm that she would be there, 6pm, that she would eat dinner if he cooked it, that she wanted to do this.

She really *didn't* want to do this, and so her affirmations were weak, and he sought further affirmations to see that she really did want to do this but, again because she didn't, they weren't forthcoming.

There was, thus, a sort of strange undertone of hostility to the day as Carrie, perhaps somewhat sadistically, stayed on the couch in her pajamas until late afternoon, laptop on her lap writing something, telling him that in a second she'd go get the mac and all the cheese and all the booze and the pies, just let her finish this.

He meanwhile was fussing over the turkey, checking the uninformative oven roughly every twenty-five minutes, making sure the potatoes soaking in water on the range hadn't spontaneously combusted or evaporated.

Eventually she went, on one of the few days really requiring a jacket, to a mildly busy Walmart full of atypical shoppers, people sent out for forgotten things or the miserable for whom this wasn't any special day. She stocked up healthily on booze, having made sure this was her beat, and then cheese and pasta and also some premade stuff in case she didn't feel like cooking.

In his absence, though, she started to mellow out and feel less annoyed, and she realized this was sort of important for him, and so she resolved to be nicer, benevolence toward others always being easier in their absence. She picked up a tatty Justin Bieber T-shirt as a sort of present/dish towel, their shared hatred of him being one of the few things which unites them.

Getting out of her car, the day almost dark, she looked up at the lighted window of their apartment and tried to arrange her face in a smile, having read that study that if you pretend to smile it lightens your mood.

—I come bearing gifts.

—Great, thanks!

He was bent over, staring into the oven.

—Think I got everything. Will I make the mac and cheese now? Or too early?

—No let me, this is my baby.

—Nah, it's ours, I'll do it. Just tell me when.

—Okay, thank you!

She felt pleased with herself that she had been nice, and went to her bedroom to recover. But it was after five, and it was a holiday, so she felt it acceptable to drink, and went out and poured herself some wine and offered it to Jordan, who refused then accepted, and sat at the breakfast nook. The turkey, she had to admit, smelled pretty fucking good.

—That turkey smells pretty fucking good. Here, have some wine. It's the holidays.

She prevailed upon him, and distraction led him to finish a glass quickly and he became almost instantly south of tipsy, and then soon worried about his lack of a clear head.

—Oh god, what am I doing, right . . .

—Chill out dude, it's just some potatoes. They can go in whenever.

—Nah, they gotta be boiled ten minutes, my mom always said it had to be like that when you make potatoes . . . but it's whatever.

—Uh, you've been on your feet all day, let me take over, I know what I'm doing.

—No, no, I'm on it, just gotta . . . echh is that wine acidy?

He turned to her, heat-flushed and wine-flushed.

—My here . . .

Pointing to his esophagus.

—Feels all acidic.

—It's coz dude you've been cooking for like six hours solid.

Did you even eat lunch today? Siddown for chrissake let me do something.

—Nah, I'll just get an antacid. We'll be done so soon, it's like thirty minutes tops.

—Okay, well I'ma start on the mac and cheese then.

—Oh shit, I'd forget! Okay, yes, please.

They swapped places, he now sitting, she now standing, overseeing. The glass of wine had pretty well shaken off the funk and she was now looking forward to eating.

—Smells goood.

She put the whole bag of cheese in with a whole thing of cream and loads of pepper, and got lost in stirring the sauce until she realized Jordan had vanished.

—Dude, where are you? We're almost done.

— . . . I'm coming. Just checking my email.

They didn't have a dining table, which somewhat hampered things, but Carrie took her desk and put it in the center of the room, and placed chairs on either side. It was a bit awkward, because there was nowhere for their legs to go, so they had to sit at right angles from the table and each other, but it had the advantage that all the eatables and drinkables could be within reach.

And so they were, now: a plate with some of the turkey, roughly hewn, bread, roast potatoes, and the mac and cheese which had turned out great. Jordan entered, looking sad.

—Look at all this.

Carrie said, now very happy, hoping she had misread his face. A weak smile disabused her of that hope.

—Happy Thanksgiving!

She went and got him the Bieber shirt, and he played the part of happy amused giftee as best he could.

—Thanks for making all this, it looks really, really great.

—Thank you.

He said, flatly. Something was obviously bothering him.

Should she say something? Like, are you okay? Or just get on with the meal, see if whatever it was would leave him?

He barely ate, and this kind of scuppered her appetite, so after around seven minutes of tense food-related pleasantries:

—What's up? Something's clearly wrong.

—It's nothing. Just missing home.

—Ah.

That was perfectly understandable. Well, kind of. From his oblique comments and most notably from the fact that he wasn't there now, Carrie had gotten the impression that home wasn't such a good place for him.

—Sorry man. Holidays are tough.

—Yeah?

—Yeah man, this is the first time I've actually done a Thanksgiving thing since I've been away. Actually apart from Dublin, funny enough.

—They have that there?

—No, but we did something.

Jordan knew all about the breakup: he had, without being bidden, scrubbed the blood from Carrie's carpet when she took Jules to the hospital. And he knew how upset she'd been in the aftermath.

—It must be so hard for you.

And he was approaching being visibly upset at—seemingly—her plight. And this made her upset at her plight too. It *was* pretty hard for her.

—You gotta just make the best, I guess. Like you've been doing! This is great, this.

He got up and got a glass of water and started walking around the kitchen area.

—Where are you?

—They don't want me there.

He said.

—Who don't? What? Nah, man, they do dude.

—They don't. They don't want me there. Not a word, no messages, nothing. Why would they?

Carrie was now quickly very angry.

—Well, fuck them! They don't know shit. Like, you may love them but fuck 'em. They're wrong. That's it. *Fuck. Them.*

—I don't want that though.

— . . . I know.

She got up and hugged him.

—You can't like blame yourself for their mistake. Maybe they'll realize. You just gotta live your own life . . .

The 'your own' was slow and stressed.

— . . . Forget about what was, like man these times, I can't help think back too, you know. Like, it's hard but sometimes that's it . . . all we can do is try and make new families, you know.

—Holidays are just . . .

—Yeah, for real, I know I know. You think back to how it was. I do that, too. Sorry if I've been a cunt today.

—No, you haven't.

For some reason that was what started him crying, and they stood there huddled together, and he sobbed into her shoulder for a while, and she could feel the air clearing. After five or ten minutes, when it seemed to have subsided:

—Holidays man, fuck 'em. Come on, let's eat turkey and pie and drink wine. That's the solution to life's problems. Seriously, it is, turkey, wine, and pie. Two orphans and holiday foods, c'mon. Like Dickens.

He laughed, snorting out snot onto her top.

—I'm not an orphan.

He said, but with more lightness in his voice.

—C'mon, let's eat. And then you can hand-wash my top.

He didn't eat then, but had a shower, having gotten sweaty from the cooking, and Carrie waited for him until he resurfaced about an hour later, and then they ate on the couch together and watched *Airplane II.*

* * *

A few days after Thanksgiving, she woke up to find a couple of the followers of her FemSoc account drawing to her attention a tweet by @rightadjacent which had, unbeknownst to her, gone viral (she hadn't logged in for a while, having come to feel like it was a bad idea, especially having seen Jordan's suffering face to face). It read:

It's not transphobic or racist or classist to think that older conservative societies lead more to happiness for it's members than today's.

It was one of her specious tweets that she thought maybe contained a grain of truth (she was naturally prone to idealise family and perhaps overestimate its importance) but was mostly wrong.

A few people who followed the FemSoc account suggested she set this person right, and so she did, pretty much using her own voice and publicly replying:

—*Even if* this is true, so what? Wrong to persecute lgbt+, immigrants, etc. Just wrong.

This in turn got retweeted a lot. Along the way, Jordan, who had a surprisingly adversarial social media persona, replied to @rightadjacent:

—*its, I guess today's society fails on education too right?

As a burn it didn't make all that much sense, but such is life. Carrie found this argument with herself somewhat amusing, but was otherwise embarrassed to see the fruits of @rightadjacent's labour showing up the real world of her and her friends. Her desire to do this shit had already steeply fallen, but now she decided it was for real enough, and logged in one last time to deactivate her account.

6

Carrie found herself in the utility room of Jordan's friend Max's large shared apartment. There was a dryer and a washer and various detergents, and she was eating from a massive bag of chips she had pretty much just stolen from the kitchen.

It was a very nice party, she had to say. Normally she would have avoided hanging out with Jordan and his friend but she realized it was another opportunity to make friends, and she had come early and helped decorate and did, indeed, seem to be getting on well with pretty much all the ten or so people here.

—Hey Carrie, this is your sort of thing.

Jordan rounded the corner into the little room unsteadily, smiling with a glazed look which one would normally attribute to drugs, but Carrie knew was just a combination of excitement and tipsiness.

—Do you know this, pantycount? Pantaccount?

He looked off to someone separated from Carrie by the wall.

—Pantact. Do you know this thing? It's really weird . . . here come on, tell her . . .

He dragged into the closet a short man with ginger brown hair and a well-tended ginger brown beard, whose features were unfortunately squashed. He was evidently uncomfortable about being paraded.

—Huh, yeah.

He began, embarrassed and notably undrunk, talking as someone who's been instructed to talk to someone about something which they have only shaky evidence that that latter someone will be interested in.

—Ah, so yeah basically, it's this time travel app, that's what they say anyway.

—Time travel? That's some app.

—Well, you know the Facebook fbi fight?

—Kind of, yeah.

He was referring to a recent issue concerning users' access to the data social media and other websites stored on them. In the summer she had graduated, there had been a furor about big data, which put tech companies and the government against each other.

It concerned two related things: firstly, the provision of a person's data to a third party in case of illness, accident or death, and second the form in which provided data came. It came to light in the case of a nineteen-year-old man with bipolar disorder. When he went missing, and wasn't quickly found, the police missing person's people wanted access to his various social media records, on which he was active. The social media companies, though, had rules in place that prevented such a thing: in the absence of an explicit statement to the effect that one bequeaths one's digital estate to another, they refused, as a matter of course, to grant access.

And so, perhaps not heeding the details of this particular case, they did so. The parents, long since accustomed to fight battles on behalf of their son, didn't take this, and their story made the papers, and, after a brief tussle, at least some of the sites relented, for this particular case, and handed it over.

But this led to problem two: what they got was nigh on unusable. While they were given the data, it was often in more or less impossible to parse form: for one site, just a several hundred kilobyte long csv spreadsheet. This was the sort of thing the right program could extract information from, of course, but not humans, and while the respective companies had offered assistance in helping them make information out of this data, this nevertheless hobbled the investigation.

When he was eventually found after five days, two hundred miles away and having slept in a hotel for four of the nights, the story had been well represented in online and print media for days, and its two aspects attracted the attention of two different sorts of people. There were some who thought that looking through a person's digital record was the same sort of thing as a detective looking through their bedroom for clues, and of course the sites should grant access to it. The others felt, in a way they struggled quite to express, that the cases were notably disanalogous, that such data bore a much more intimate relation to a person, a relation that went far beyond that of a 'clue', and that to give over the data was, in a certain sense, to give over the person.

This was a complex philosophical debate conducted by non-philosophers, and conducted poorly (philosophers themselves got very interested in it, but they mostly were ignored by the general public). As such, it was soon swept out of most people's minds.

But it kindled an interest in the matter of a person's access to the data stored about them. Abstracting from complex cases involving impairment, it had long been the case that a person was entitled to the data a website stored about them. But this entitlement didn't extend to the data being provided in a tractable form. It was argued that it was a fundamental right not merely to let people have access to the data if they so wished, but that there be an accessible centralized repository of this data. In the absence of this, the asymmetry between one's access to data and others' was too great: it was pointless to grant a user access to their data without also granting them a way to manipulate it, in roughly the same way that one could have cause for complaint if it were given to one as binary.

—Well, these guys have made an app to sort of deal with that: it collects up all your data and lets you search it.

So continued squashed-face.

—Oh, cool.

—Yeah, but like the really cool thing is it allows this feature they call time travelling: you put in a date, and it will replay, in real time, all your Internet activity: searches, texts, Facebook, news sites, all that. It's like digital time travel.

—Fuck, that sounds like fun.

—I knew you'd like it!

Jordan's face came from behind the wall, where he had evidently, for some reason, been listening.

—It's like personal identity, all that stuff, right? Like what is the relation between a person and their info? What do you think?

—I think dude, I don't wanna talk to a wall, come here man. Yeah, super, super interesting.

* * *

The next day, having arranged a date with the only other straight person at the party for the weekend, Carrie happily looked into pantact some more. It turned out, as you might imagine, that the whole thing was a big con to get data. Although billed as a fight for personal liberty against powerful companies, in using pantact one was in essence signing over all one's data to its makers, which enabled much more accurately targeted ads, and thus ads which advertisers would pay more for.

Say, for example, you had a user who talks about Buñuel on Facebook and *True Detective* on Twitter. With that combined information, to a greater degree of accuracy, one can predict that such a person would like *Twin Peaks*, and that accordingly an ad directing them to buy *Twin Peaks* would have a greater chance of being successful.

Carrie was fascinated by pantact, and especially by the 'time travel' feature that let you replay all your Internet activity from a given day in the past. She'd been reading about the way various technologies or changes in forms of life change the nature of the human. Think, for example, of a land-locked community which suddenly comes to acquire horses, and thus the ability to traverse much larger stretches of ground. This gives birth, according to anthropologists working in horse studies, to a new sort of being:

the centaur, half-person, half-horse. Or think of how we rely on Facebook to store information about other people's birthdays. For philosophers, this leads to a new sort of thing: an *extended* mind, a mind not merely localized inside a skull. She thought, maybe, the same thing was going on here: as horses extend one's spatial reach, so pantact extends one's temporal reach into the past. She started thinking about trying to write a blog post or something about it, tying it up with her own work on identity. To do that, though, she thought she better try out the app, and so signed up, uploading a lot of information and using, with a twinge, a caricature of her as a character from *The Simpsons* which Jules had got her as a gift. She couldn't use it immediately, though, as it took several days for the app to retrieve all one's data from the different sites it was stored on.

The day after that, she woke from a dreamless twelve-hour sleep still alive with the idea, and went to the library, planning in her head on the bus already the text of her blog, having conversations in her head with the party dude she was going to see next week.

* * *

—C'monnnn Carrie, we got to go.

She had just popped home to pick up her charger, and had been met by a panicked Jordan. He had texted her earlier worried, saying that he *really* needed to speak to her, things were fucked up, but she didn't take this particularly seriously (the last time he *really* needed to speak to her their cable had gone out and he had drawn the catastrophizing conclusion that his or her bank account had been emptied and the service thus cancelled), and had put her phone in her bag, and then later when she was a bit drunk and out in the night air smoking, she saw she had a bunch of missed calls and phoned him back, but when he didn't pick up she completely forgot, and got on with her date, which had gone very well. Zach was back in the bar now, waiting for her; they were going to his place.

—They're going to kill me, they know where I live.

—What, who?

—Some guys, they emailed me, told me I'd threatened someone, I needed to pay.

—Threatened? You?

—Come on, I packed some stuff, sorry I hope you don't mind, Max said we can stay.

—Wait, what. Just wait. What.

—They have my address, we gotta leave now, I've been waiting for hours, we're ready to go. Come *onnnn* we can't stay here.

—Who, what?

—That girl, the girl you argued with, they said I'd scared her off, was a bully, said they're going to tell my family some shit . . . and come here.

—What girl? I didn't argue with anybody.

—On Twitter, the girl, the right-wing girl, the eye one.

Carrie stood confused, trying to process through the information, noticing the three packed bags and the laptop in a pile in the middle of the room.

—The girl threatened you? No, that can't be.

—No, not her, her friends or whatever, said I'd been rude and needed to pay. That I'd trolled her and made her leave the site.

—But she doesn't . . .

—What?

—Nothing . . . and they emailed you?

—Yes, with this address, said they were gonna like . . . bother my parents, all that.

—How did they get this address?

Now she was starting to get worried. They had got the address laughably easily, as Jordan's full name, picture, and university affiliation were tied to his account, and his phone number was tied to his Facebook which didn't have particularly adequate privacy settings.

—I don't know, who knows what these computer people can do.

Carrie paused, and thought.

—I'm not going. These fucking guys are all talk. Why would you even think they're around here? These douchebags, they're probably hundreds of miles away. I gotta go dude, but just stay here.

—No, absolutely not. I can't. It's faaar too risky. And you can't stay here either.

—Fine, well you go, I'm not going.

The only reason she hadn't brought Zach here was out of consideration for Jordan, but if he wasn't going to be here . . .

—No, no absolutely not. I couldn't live with myself if I got you in trouble. I just couldn't. You have to come. Max even said you could have his bed, we can stay as long as we want.

—Nothing's going to happen, dude. Look, c'mon, let's just chill a bit.

—We have to go.

And Carrie vacillated. There were two paths open to her: she could reveal the truth, and thereby presumably alienate Jordan quite seriously. Or she could lie and go and hide out indefinitely in some shithole away from her TV and bed and in the company of Jordan and his weird friend. It still wasn't *quite* getting through to her that she was possibly in real danger: the whole thing was too pregnated with unreality, given @ rightadjacent's non-existence. But she felt she couldn't admit the whole embarrassing thing, and so, wearily, she said:

—I better get my fucking toothbrush. But look, I'm going to stay with Zach.

They were making, about thirty minutes later, one of two trips down the stairs, Jordan not really getting the packing light concept, when Carrie halted.

—Listen, man. You don't have to.

—Nah, I have to. And I'd really prefer it if you went with me, I don't think I'll feel safe if I don't know where you are tonight. I'm so sorry for getting you into this.

Looking down at him, pitiful, Carrie groaned.

—Awww fuck.

Realizing she'd made a decision. She told him. He left. He completely failed to understand it—it was literally incomprehensible to him why someone would do that, and his vacant confusion made Carrie feel uneasy about herself. The other's bafflement made her baffled: why *had* she done all this?

—But that person . . . that was a horrible person?

—Right. Don't know what to tell you.

She was beginning to feel the anger you feel to someone you wronged.

—But you can't stay here.

He was confused, now at the bottom of the external staircase she was halfway up.

—Told you, I'm going to Zach's.

But now she doubted that she *was* going to Zach's, who was somehow closely connected to Max, and who would surely find out sooner rather than later.

—But anyway look, even if they come, which they won't, like they're not gonna bother a lady.

She said, optimistically. He looked up at her. She shrugged. He walked away. She went back in the apartment, paced around, wondering was there, could there be, people out there watching her? Preparing to attack the friend of the person who alienated their non-existent friend?

She doubted it, really. Again, the chances they'd actually be in New Orleans were quite slim. But she felt the air once again full of that fear she had never really gotten rid of, the fear that violence permeates the fabric of the everyday, waiting to flash up when least expected. Pacing, she didn't know what the fuck to do and thought about running away or getting a hotel or securing the door somehow. But most of all she thought again of the fragility of bodies.

7

About five thousand miles away, about one month earlier, Jules walked up the chilly stairs of his father's house to the unlit first floor hall. At its far end a window let in moonlight. There was the smell of soap, more noticeable in the dark, and the sound of the hot water tank filling or emptying.

He turned the light on and the moonlight disappeared and he, a dark figure surrounded by electric yellow, replaced it. Cropped hair and an untidy beard had been replaced by a mass of moustache and sideburns and beard and long unkempt hair, making him look like an IRA leader of the 70s and successfully masking the inherent geekiness of his face. He looked to make sure the path to his room was unobstructed and turned the light back off and walked in dark, then entered the room.

His computer was the sole source of brightness there, and even it was black, except the caps lock key and the battery indicator. He touched the tracker and the screen came up. There was, as he expected there might be, one new order waiting for him. He copied the address into a word document, upped the font, and printed it. There was the quiet crinkle followed by the whirring and then the shunt of paper being fed in, printed on, and out. He took the printed paper and got scissors and cut around the text, and then got an envelope from his top drawer and cut pieces of tape from a roll and fixed the paper to the envelope.

Then he had a second thought: he hadn't got a screenshot showing any donation, and couldn't remember having given the customer the link to the Gofundme. He double-checked, bringing up the message thread with the customer to get his ID.

—So they're four, yeah?

—Yeah, I think so. Definitely not too messy, although maybe more than the photo. The account is bit.ly/ssash :)

—That's fine!

He clicked through and saw a recent donation of €16, an atypical amount he asked for as a sort of double check in case someone tried to falsify a screenshot.

So he raised from his computer and put the underwear, already pre-sealed in a clear bag, in the envelope, and then, having struggled with the tape a bit, sealed the bag over, and put it in his rucksack, in which another sealed envelope lay, ready to take to the post office tomorrow.

With the aim of creating a revolution in morality, Jules had been selling used underwear for the past two weeks. It was pretty simple: he ate food and drank drinks, he digested and then excreted what he consumed, the process of excretion made underwear messy, and people paid for messy underwear.

The whole revolution in morality thing was based on the idea that people are neither good nor bad, but that they are what others around them are. Surrounded by good, one is good; surrounded by bad, one is bad. So if you could surround a given person with good, they'd be good: goodness is self-perpetuating in that way. The problem, though, was starting off the whole procedure: getting the first good people to make the others good. People were naturally selfish.

But people were other things: lustful, for example. Jules was harnessing the lustfulness to overcome the selfishness: he gave away the underwear provided the buyers promised to do good deeds. So far, it was going well, and he was quietly satisfied at the thought that he was making the world a better place.

Of course, it wasn't completely straightforward. As far as he could tell, there wasn't so strong a market for men's underwear, and so he had to pretend to be a woman both on the site and, to some extent, in real life: he had to wear women's underwear and, worrying about somehow exuding a male air, he started using female products in the shower, sneaking them in and out and confusing, mildly, the nose of his father. And he had to tell a range of lies and misrepresent himself, abusing the trust of others. And if he were to get found out, it would be very embarrassing.

He wouldn't have done all this if he didn't believe he was doing something good. But he thought that he was, and that enabled him to overcome the material inconveniences and the guilt that telling all these lies caused. He thought of himself as an engineer fixing up the broken system of morality, controlling these men and causing them to be, in little ways, better, and hoping that their improvement would yield improvement in others around them. This deeply held belief about the structure of the moral world and his capacity to change it is what pushed him through, as now, when he was getting a new order ready.

He began this strange path around September of the autumn after New Orleans. It was a very bad time. The preceding months had been hectic: coming back to Dublin stung with disappointment, he had no time to brood, going straight into a schedule of classes and coursework and then exams interspersed with doctor's and dentist's appointments, now suddenly without the person who had been there every day the whole of the previous year.

Things got worse after finals. He didn't do anywhere near as well as he had hoped. This meant, admittedly, he only got a high two one instead of a high first, but he was hugely disappointed. The micromicrotransaction project had received a very poor grade, the external examiner having pointed out that microtransactions were at present barely financially viable and that micromicrotransactions definitely weren't. He knew this, of course, but also thought that financial unviability surely didn't count against a project's feasibility, as witness literally any big tech company struggling with monetisation.

Soon he found himself back in his father's house full-time, for the first time since he was eighteen, cramped, depressed, and lonely. He started duly applying for jobs, thinking at least he would soon be able to leave—he still had a decent computer science degree, and Ireland was big for that. But no: the summer rolled on, and he woke and applied for jobs and ate dinner with his father then watched movies in bed, every single day, and nothing transpired. He found himself quickly eating through his meagre savings, and so around August resigned himself to the possibility that this could be his life for a while and signed on the dole.

But after a month of that, a month of traipsing across town for special classes on how to write CVs led by people who would hypercorrect his English, and filling in applications for jobs he didn't want and wasn't wanted for, it was felt his performance wasn't adequate, and he needed to go on JobPath, essentially an unpaid internship scheme, but ostensibly for the developing of real-world business skills.

He was paired with Home Start, a homelessness charity. This involved him spending a lot of time in the tiny little front room of a church, which functioned as the main hub for the charity: it was the place they had regular dinners at, where they cooked the food that they brought out onto the streets, where they held the NA and AA meetings, and so on. JobPath was, he thought, a typical neo-liberal scam: forcing people to do unpaid work to make up for the woeful social security system. But he needed the money, so he resentfully resigned himself to it. And it was at JobPath that he got the idea for the underwear scam, from a girl named Sara.

* * *

—Silent nights great, but I'd much rather be making sandwiches with youuu.

—Don't worry, don't worry, I told them the situation, they understood, said they'd sign you in. They know what's up . . . anyway I'm making sandwiches enough for two.

He was. Sitting on a round step stool with wheels, he was

hunched over a table just big enough for a plate, a loaf of shitty white bread, some value ham, cheese, and a yellow spread. On one half of the plate were the made sandwiches and on the other one in progress. The vicinity smelled like bad ham air.

From his vantage point in the room, which was just at that time of the day when it's slightly too early to turn on the lights, but the natural light is more or less done—in effect the darkest hour of the day, squat in the afternoon—he saw a chair in the centre of the room, bony bare elbows beside it, long greasy hair above it.

A man facing him looked down at the occupant seriously, whose elbows' motion suggested he was speaking. A gruff, low sound occasionally made its way over to Jules, and at one point the occupant turned to Jules and smiled weakly, raising his hand in greeting.

—You're so good.

—De nada.

—So listen, I'm thinking, he's GOT to take Curtis this weekend, especially after this . . . like I just texted his mum and ofc, she said fuck all but I know she'll get on to him about it.

Sara was at a carol school rehearsal with her son, Curtis, which his father was meant to have taken him to. He was more or less a deadbeat, someone who she claimed worked just little enough to not have to pay child support and who frequently—as today—cancelled when he was meant to spend time with his son.

They had been split for two years, essentially just after Curtis was born. Sara had managed, with the help of her family, to keep up a job and a young child by herself until recently, when the job's hours were cut, and she found herself back at home, on the dole and attending the same JobStart program as Jules.

It was this similarity between them that, despite their different places in life and the age difference (she was about a decade older than him), had brought them together. They bonded over

Larry David and obscure Netflix documentaries, Jules realizing, to his surprize, that mothers were people too, and soon after that he was attracted to her. And Sara, despite having qualms about the age gap, was pleased to have someone roughly eligible in her life for the first time in at least three years: if Kris, the father, was ever eligible, he certainly wasn't during that last year they were together.

They thus drifted together quickly, and at a casual coffee after the church one Friday morning they swapped phone numbers, and this led to texting and the arranging, often thwarted, of going to see a film, which ended with them kissing for an extended period on the outside of St. Stephen's Green, something they stopped only and with reluctance when a teenage boy threw half a can of coke at them.

—So we could get a hotel?

—Yeah? I've never got a hotel in Dublin before.

—Well, clearly our places are out . . .

—Clearly. . . . —I'm down, I'll look? Tho I have very little money.

—That's okay, as long as he does the right thing, I have some money I was going to use this weekend on Curtis, so . . .

—Okay, well next time my treat . . . anyway we can go cheap, right?

—Yeah, as long as it's got a bed I'm happy ;)

—Me too . . . —I assure you that despite the absence of a winky emoji you should read an equal amount of salaciousness into my reply.

—!! —hahaha, you really know how to talk to women — Anyway GREAT, we can go to dinner and maybe the cinema again? or the theatre? and some drinks . . . arrrggggh! it's been so long since I've had a date!

—I'm sure it's difficult.

—You have no idea. You better bring your A game mister, I want flowers and please please shave and also, do you even have any nice clothes?

—I will, you got it, but I'm cultivating a bohochic look here, ehhhhhhh (respectively).

—haha! good. Fun fun.

Jules made another sandwich, and then continued the conversation:

—Mal's here again.

—Yeah? —Poor guy.

—Yeah.

—What's he talking about?

—I don't know, I'm here buttering.

—I feel so sorry for him.

—Yeah . . . do you know what his deal his? I can never hear him too good . . .

—Nah, I don't know. Definitely in recovery, I'd guess heroin to look at him. He's got mouth problems.

—Tell me about it, it's hard to talk to him . . . his teeth make me feel squirmy, and I find I don't hear what he says because I'm so concentrated on making sure my eyes don't go to his mouth . . . you know?

There was a bit of a pause. Jules really was driven crazy by this guy's teeth. His lower incisors were entirely, immaculately black. No spots of white shone through: it looked like they were painted. And so it looked like the man was harbouring this inorganic, perhaps plastic, matter in the centre of his face, and this made it very difficult for Jules to understand and empathize with him, just as it's difficult to understand and empathize with patio furniture.

—I guess . . . he's had a hard life. I think it's inspiring that he's still going.

—Yeah me too, I was thinking maybe I'd set up a Gofundme for him, for his medical bills? Do you think people would contribute?

—I don't know . . . but it's a nice idea . . . gtg somebody's giving me the evil eye for texting in church . . . look for hotels you, can't wait for the weekend, it's going to be so much fun! Can't wait to finally get my hands on that body young man ;)

* * *

—So do you want to have children yourself, Jules?

Said Sara's gran.

—Gran! For fuck . . .

Said Sara.

—Sara!

Said Sara's mum.

—No.

Said Jules.

He was keenly aware of three generations of mothers staring at him, and felt he better continue. As, unfortunately, he did.

— Well, um, maybe, you know arguably given the scarcity of natural resources it's actually immoral to procreate, but . . .

He was now keenlier aware of the Kennedy family's many maternal eyes on him and started to redden.

—Although I'm sure whenever you were . . . deciding whether or not to have children, I mean, that was a different era.

And at this last, Sara pitied him, got up from the sofa where she was sitting in between her mother and her grandmother, and came and sat on the armchair's armrest beside him. In a slightly northside accent she rescued him:

—Leave him alone you pair, poor guy wasn't expecting this, were you?

The weekend plans had fallen in. They had done so, in fact, very soon after their text conversation: Sara had requested that Kris take the child, and he had refused.

It was disappointing, but they had settled on a contingency plan for the following Wednesday: Sara's mother and grandmother were going to be out of the house, so they arranged a midmorning booty call. But they were barely in the door from a rough Dublin day, in Sara's gran's chintzy front room, when a key was heard in the door and generations materialized.

—So you'll stay for lunch, anyway?

Asked Sara then added, quietly, 'sure you're here now'. Jules smiled tightly, as unviable excuses cascaded through his head, before agreeing. Sara and her mum went into the kitchen to prepare food, telling Jules and the grandmother to make conversation. And Jules seemingly took to the task readily, asking the gran if she wanted him to change the messed-up aspect ratio on the TV which she had instinctively turned on when sitting down.

The gran had an exceptional appetite, so they tended to have a full meal at lunch, and Sara and her mum set about making potatoes and gammon. About to put the latter in the oven, Sara thought she better check—she realized now it had never come up—if Jules ate meat, and so went back into the living room to ask him.

—But you see the problem is that humans are essentially bad.

She heard Jules saying from the threshold. She entered. Jules was leaning forward, concentrating and looking at his shoes. Gran was sitting back, her shrunk frame tiny in the large big-cushioned sofa, her white hair easily missable against the white fabric, smiling mildly. She had been politely inquiring about the church charity, and its problems.

—That's why these things are needed. You can't trust people to do good.

Sara quickly interrupted Jules, asking him as to his preferences when it comes to meat, and telling them both that they shared their alma mater, in an effort to change the topic. It didn't take.

—So really I think, to be honest, you have to force people to do good.

She was getting very worried that he'd break out the 'forced labour for good camp' thought he had shared with her on their first coffee date.

—Ah now, shouldn't force people. People have to find their own way.

Said the gran, announcing the platitude merrily and looking up to Sara for her approval. Sara smiled back.

—Well yeah, ideally like but it's not happening. But this is what could happen, I think . . . it's very frustrating because, actually, I misspoke when I said people are *essentially* bad.

Sara felt a bit relieved.

—No, they're *accidentally* bad but they're *essentially* sheep—they do what those around them do. People are bad because they're surrounded by bad. I'm bad because you're bad, you're bad because she's bad, and so on.

The grandmother took the news that she was bad with equanimity.

—But, like, conversely, people would be good if they were surrounded by good. I'd be good if you were, and so on.

Sara had been neglecting the potatoes, watching the conversation unfold, waiting for a chance to butt in.

—Ah, 'would' c'mon! She is good, you can't be coming here dissing my granny!

—No, I'm sure she is, I mean in the abstract like.

—Well abstract, this isn't the time for abstract. Nan did English too. This one did some English, right?

—Yeah, I sat in on an English class.

—You ever read George Eliot? She likes George Eliot.

This managed to divert the conversation; as she went back to the kitchen, the grandmother was beginning what sounded like a well-told tale about Eliot's clashes with the society of her time. Sara hastily put the gammon in the oven, the potato pan on a rolling boil, and rushed back to the living room, just in time to hear:

—Honestly, I'd be perfectly willing to torture someone with my own bare hands if it were to save enough lives.

The conversation had moved from Eliot to the decline of theism to the rise of science, to the rise of utilitarianism to, inexorably, bare-handed torture.

—Broccoli or beans?

8

—Fucking selfish pricks is what the problem is.

—Who?

—People.

—Ah c'mon, you can't expect them, we're all broke like.

—I have two hundred Facebook friends, you have the same, Danielle has the same, fucking Rupert has near a thousand. Sixty euro. C'mon like. Selfish pricks.

—It's really sweet that you're doing it for him. You've done your best. And like, it's not nothing.

—It'll get him what? One doctor's appointment. Or dentist appointment, I guess. Do you know, what he's in for? Like what's wrong with him?

Sara shrugged.

—You've never asked him?

—Sure you know yourself he barely talks, poor guy. I think he must be in constant pain with his teeth. Feel so sorry for him.

—Aye, but what good is feeling sorry for him? Does *no* good.

—Well, you can help in other ways than the Gofundme. We were going to go visit him next Sunday. Come with us. Then we can go for dinner afterward, my ma won't mind looking after Curtis a couple of hours.

That was exactly what he didn't want to do. It's very hard to visit someone whom you can't look at. And he couldn't look at Mal. He felt it must surely be evident, his discomfort, and how must that make him feel, to have someone avoiding eye contact like that? Better it was to hide in the corner on his computer, help him as he knows how.

But evidently he didn't know how to help. He had set up the Gofundme and tried to promote it, but so far it had been doing extremely poorly. It was just so frustrating. If every social media contact which they shared were to donate one euro that would be close to two grand, and it would cost the people nothing. But people just didn't give a fuck.

—Fucking . . . fuckers.

It was dark outside, and smelled of coffee. Naturally, because it was late afternoon in winter and they were in a coffee shop. Already evening traffic on College Green was busy, students were streaming out of Trinity and Christmas lights were tracing the shape of a tree before it.

Jules was tautly caffeinated, feeling tense and full of gloom, having spent the afternoon going from coffee shop to coffee shop, buying coffee out of obligation, filling in applications for jobs he probably wouldn't get, refreshing the Gofundme, and hating humanity. Then Sara had texted him unexpectedly looking to meet up and he couldn't think of a reason to put her off again.

Things had kind of fizzled since the booty call manqué/intergenerational lunch. Sara's schedule again became packed, and they reacted in seemingly opposing ways to this. Her interest was dulled in no way by the fact they couldn't get together: she texted him every day, even as his replies became more spread apart and less conversation-continuing, pressing forward, dropping some quite major hints that she would like to get a couple of cheap Ryanair tickets one weekend and visit Rome, where she had friends and visits regularly.

Jules felt hemmed in by this, that he seemed somehow to have found himself in the trappings of a relationship without any of the benefits, and had been trying to extricate himself from the situation. But he found it difficult, partly from the natural unpleasantness such things occasion, but also because he got the sense that her interest in him wasn't really an interest in *him*, but just an interest in the first halfway eligible person who had stumbled across her path. And he shared with her the desire that she find some halfway eligible person. He would just rather it wasn't him.

So, like any mature person, he was aiming just to be low-key mean and distant enough to her until she got the message. And that meant consenting to meet her now. He was worried, though. She had been obliquely referring to something she needed to talk about with him, and he feared that she was going to suggest taking their—to him non-existent—relationship to the next level.

—So listen, there's one thing I need to tell you, if we're going to continue dating.

He was struck dumb by her presupposition that they were dating, but 'We're not dating' sounded so harsh. He hoped maybe she'd say something that would give him an out.

—It's like . . . remember you'd wondered where I got the money to take me and Curtis to Amsterdam last month?

—Uh-huh.

—Well, see I've got this kind of side venture. So don't be mad. Okay?

—I won't be.

—Well see basically, there's this site, loads of people use it, where you can sell things.

—Yeah that's eBay.

—No, like, well, basically I sell my used underwear . . . it's such easy money, like. People pay good. No work. You know I can't rely on anything else for money, these fuckers—

She pointed roughly in the vicinity of the church, but he knew she meant the social services.

—Nor Kris, and I can hardly impose on my ma. That's why I do it, it's nothing . . . well, say something!

—So wait, like . . . the money's good?

—Pretty good. And it doesn't do anyone any harm, really?

She smiled, thinking that he saw things her way.

—But like, there's a demand?

—There's a demand alright. I'm a MILF, yanno?

—That . . . adds value?

—Fuck yeah. Not as good as actively pregnant like.

—You did it already then?

—No! Only since I moved back and needed money. Recently. But I browse like.

—Ah.

—You're not mad?

—I wish I could fucking do it.

He was only really half-joking. She laughed.

—I knew you'd understand. So it's not a problem?

And here he paused. It wasn't a problem. He admired her use of her resources to deal with the hand life had dealt her. But he couldn't help realize this provided him a perfect out. He tried to make a sort of downcast face.

—I don't know, this is kind of a shock.

—Oh . . . it freaks you out?

—I don't know, yeah, maybe.

He felt himself rouging. He wasn't a particularly good liar.

—Need to think about it . . . I need to think, I can't pretend I'm not a bit freaked out, I'm not a particularly good liar.

Maybe he *was* a particularly good liar.

—Well I'll stop, right away. No problem. You're the only man I want around my panties.

—No! I mean, like, I don't know maybe . . . you shouldn't stop. Just let me . . .

They left on equivocal terms, and he continued his move of trying to get away from her. After a couple of days she duly got pissed off and asked him what's wrong, and he told her that he was seriously weirded out by her revelation, and maybe they should take a break. This was ridiculous: there was nothing to break, but he was happy to briefly accept there was in order to end it. She got quiet and apologized, and he was very magnanimous about it, noting how she was under pressure and it was a hard situation and he didn't judge, it's just he felt weird, and about one's feelings what can one do?

Lying by text was much easier than face to face, and although he felt a mild guilt about letting her think that he had broken up with her because of the underwear thing, he thought it was perhaps better than her knowing the alternative, and when they broke contact shortly thereafter, he was happy. Indeed, he felt good about himself: if post-Carrie life was almost banging MILFs with few repercussions, he was glad to be living post-Carrie life.

* * *

About a week later, pleased to be free of Sara, Jules was about to text Sara. He had remained frustrated and irritated with the failure of his Gofundme. He felt he was so tantalisingly close, that his plan was just being ruined by this bug in people, by their shortsighted selfishness which was like an absent semicolon preventing compilation. He wanted to debug, to force them to cease being selfish, to be good.

It wouldn't matter if they didn't really *want* to be good. If he could force some people to be good, then the goodness, he thought, would be contagious: it would spread from them to others, from their forced goodness genuine goodness would arrive, as something coming from nothing. The thought captivated him.

He found himself repeatedly assailed by an image: people as nodes in a network spread across the globe, seen from above, represented by bulbs, and he saw first one bulb go on and then an adjacent one, and then an adjacent one, and this happening in patches all over, as he gradually moved farther into space, and the whole became one light, as goodness passed from one person to another.

The trouble was switching on the nodes, getting the first people to turn away from the selfishness that is typically a person's first instinct. If you did that, the herd instinct that makes people act like those around them could kick in. But to get past that first instinct in those first people—that took power, the power of a God or a parent or something to determine people's behaviour.

He had no power to determine people's behaviour. The constant stream of 'Dear applicant, Thank you for your application. Unfortunately . . .'s in his inbox made him acutely aware of this. He had nothing people wanted, so there was no reason for people to heed him. But Sara. He thought she did, in her own way, have some small ability to determine people's behaviour. She had something, namely underwear, people wanted. He had a proposal for her: that she offer her customers a slight discount in exchange for a) making a donation to the Gofundme and b) spreading the word about it.

The idea was beautiful to him: in donating, her customers would help Mal. In spreading the word, they would cause others to help too. But more than that: in doing it, they would function as the nodes in the network that shine on first, and their goodness, even if caused by lust, would breed pure goodness in the others. It would be alchemy, turning literal shit into morality. He was going to text Sara his proposal. She cared for Mal, cared for people. He suspected she'd probably go for it.

But he tarried. Partly he didn't want to contact her again. Partly, he thought, she has her own financial issues to deal with and it would surely be asking too much for her to neglect her son for his scheme. He picked up and put down the phone again and again, deciding eventually to go for a walk to try to decide what, if anything, he should do.

He was in from a cold Dublin day, crossing the threshold of the Rathmine's Tesco, hot air being blown on him for above, when the epiphany hit him that he didn't need Sara, because he could do it himself!

Who would know? Like, surely, if he were to pretend to be a woman, no one would find out? What he'd do was set up an account, but instead of charging, ask for charitable donations. The men would do them, would set an example for others, and would feel better about themselves. Then after a wee while he'd quit, having made this tiny little improvement in the fabric of reality. There was nothing to lose, really: in the worst case he'd get caught and it would be mildly embarrassing, but the pretence made him think that he could avoid the stigma that would attach to a woman in this situation.

Walking home that evening he felt giddy with power: giddy with the sense, walking among the Trinity students going to or from town, that he could make things better, using his brains and resourcefulness to turn these empty weeks and months into something positive, make something of this nothing time.

And so that evening he started doing some research into the second-hand underwear biz. He couldn't very well ask Sara which site she used, and he noted that a preponderance of them were American, and feared that the shipping would ruin his overheads. There were no Irish ones, unsurprisingly enough, but eventually he found one catering to the British market. He was slightly worried about An Post's somewhat stringent regulations concerning what can be exported by mail, but he felt that perhaps the vagaries of import/export law were at present the least of his concerns.

That evening, as he ate his dinner, he was formulating a plan. His father was talking beans.

—They've stopped doing the tinned kidney beans in Dunnes. Only in a carton now, same price and half the size.

—Oh really, that's annoying.

(So, I'll need a source for woman's underwear, and I'm assuming people might look askance at me if I were to buy it in the shop. So, online.)

— Was going to make a chili sin carne for tomorrow but not sure now.

—Maybe Lidl might have some? They're pretty good as far as the old legumes

(but I can hardly get them sent here . . .)

— . . . go

—No, I looked in Lidl.

—Hmmm, you could try online?

(but I could get them sent to granny's house)

—Online, for beans?

—Modern era, you can get everything online these days.

(and then I'm going to need envelopes, and I assume some sort of sealed inner container. It could be expensive)

—But I guess tins probably aren't the cheapest thing to ship.

—Online for beans, you're mad.

(and also will I be able to carry out such an enterprise from here at home? Will he not notice? . . .)

—When's your reading group again?

(I can do things when his reading group is on.)

—Tuesdays. Do you not notice me not being here?

—Of course, I just don't notice which day it is you're not here.

—Hmm, head in the clouds.

—Head in the jobs.ie more like.

—I assume there's no news.

—No.

(So, get the stuff sent to granny's, pick up and return some time when he's out, then batch send on Tuesdays? Will that work?)

—Why don't you buy the dried beans and whatever, rehydrate them or whatever it is one does?

(Is there not a demand for freshness? Like, a sort of sell by date? Maybe it's like wine, just gets better with age)

—Well that's what I will do. But still, not very good.

(but maybe there's an option for express delivery or something. Which would mean I couldn't wait.)

—Yeah I guess that takes a lot of time, you need to plan ahead.

—Yeah.

(Wait a second, how am I going to explain the fact that I don't have blood-stained pants for sale?)

—The mashed potato is nice. Is there much butter in it?

—What? No, sure I'm off the dairy? There's some stock

though. Low fat. Good isn't it?

(I guess I could just say to each person that demand outstrips supply?)

—Aye, but is there not plenty of sodium then?

(Wait, doesn't the pill stop periods? Or is it the opposite, and it causes massive ones? It's one of the two . . . I really need to do some research here.)

—A bit.

—It seems to me that these low-fat dishes often replace salt with fat.

(Okay, I better google to make sure the chemical composition of male and female excrement is the same, at least barring laboratory analysis.)

9

Jules anxiously opened the email and clicked on the link and joy loosened his heart when he saw the message: 'Came today, thanks!!'

It was his first bit of feedback from his first order. Had you told him about a month ago that that stimulus would provoke that response, he certainly wouldn't have believed you. But here he was. It had been an odd week.

He had decided to take the plunge soon after the idea came to him. He had no sense of the many different ways it go could wrong, but he thought he'd start and see how far it went. And the thing was, when he actually came to do it, it seemed to involve a series of discrete steps none of which was particularly interesting: most involved using a computer, and the few that didn't involved parcels.

First, he got the underwear. He got them online, as he had planned, going, in order to keep his overheads low, for a multipack which balanced comfort with style and set him back only 12 euro for 5 (it also messed somewhat with his *recommended purchases for you*, but that was unavoidable). At the same time, he set up his account as a vendor on the website.

He had feared that there may be stringent checks in place—after all, surely he wasn't the first person to think of pulling this scam—but there were not. At first, he didn't think there was much need to create a particularly robust alter ego, but he changed his mind. He feared that if he didn't have a character in mind he might find himself somehow resorting to malenesses of speech or behaviour that might tip people off. And the only non-male he really knew, excluding family, was Carrie, so he duly set himself up as 'carryon', a feminist English student just back from studying abroad in Louisiana, needing money as her degree had just ended. The way she spoke was still fresh in his mind and he tried to pattern his communications on hers. This strange impersonation made him feel somewhat close to her and he found himself still annoyed, slightly, that she hadn't tried to get back in contact all this time, but he thought it was probably for the best; plenty more fish in the sea, as Sara had shown.

The next stage was to resolve the problem about the fact that what products he could offer was biologically circumscribed. He tried to think of a reason why he couldn't offer bloody underwear, but failed, and opted instead just to say that they were out of stock, and that he'd cross that bridge when he came to it.

After that, it was just time to wait for an order to come. And that took some time. The site had something like a dating site set-up which enabled you to see your visitors; the men had their own profile, and often adorned it with personal details, and he noted with increasing vexation and the strangest instance of jealousy that although people visited his page, no one had yet bought anything.

Further exploring revealed the site had a forum in which reviews of products could be placed, and this gave him an indication of why he hadn't had success so far: it seems that building up a name was important. And also he was quite hampered, he guessed, by the fact that he couldn't offer videos, or pictures, or Skype chat, or anything like that.

He contemplated putting up a picture he'd found on the Internet, but he feared reverse image search or something like that could cause problems. So what he did was add to his profile, indicating that he was new, that he would start to offer Skype et al. once he'd got a new computer.

He *still* got nothing, and he was all set to call it a bum deal, satisfied at least all it had cost him was a few euro. The picture thing bothered him, though. He felt that was what it was. And so he made a concession. He remembered that he had once sent Carrie, as a small present, a picture of her drawn like a character from *The Simpsons*. He found it and checked her social media (with a twinge of longing) and reverse image searched it and saw that she hadn't posted it anywhere, or if she had it wasn't googleable, and so put it up, with a note to the effect that he felt shy about revealing herself to the Internet world at the moment.

A couple of days later, a dull Sunday he had spent reading, an order came, waking him up with anxiety. It came from someone called derrytogalai, and his profile revealed him to be, indeed, from Ireland's Derry. A thought struck him: *that* could be a differentiating characteristic. Authentic *Irish* knickers. He planned to modify his profile accordingly, with references to Guinness and clovers and peat.

He told derrytogalai that for payment he should just donate a discretionary amount to the Gofundme, and then send a screen shot and an online receipt confirming that he had done so. That evening he set to work. He put on the fresh pair of the underwear. It was a bit snug, but he was willing to suffer through that for the greater good. And then he waited. The next day he managed not quite so obsessively to check the site, going about his daily business. But he was dismayed, at the end of the day, to notice that there was really very little indication of wear. He hadn't quite anticipated that failure of hygiene would be so difficult.

He realized that these things take time, but at the same time he didn't want to keep derrytogalai waiting. So he tried to expedite the procedure. That was a truly horrible disaster which made his hands stink for the rest of the evening and so he decided that slow and steady was necessary. By Wednesday afternoon they were ready, and he sent them off first class.

Then began the waiting. Just as he had worried about other people being in on the scam, so he worried that the users would have some preternatural ability to discern that his was sham product, and that he would, any day, get an email denouncing him. Accordingly, he made sure, when confirming that he'd posted, to ask derrytogalai to confirm he'd received and that he was happy with the product. And so he had waited tensely a couple of days, during which time another order came in, until he received, with the joy mentioned, derrytogalai's confirmation. It had started.

* * *

Like a heavy sack, Malcolm was lying motionless on the raised part of the hall, his boots facing the room, the only part of him visible.

He was in a lot of pain, and hadn't been sleeping, and, fearing opiates, had no adequate anaesthetic. His motionless feet darkened the already dark room, as people whispered what was to be done.

—Aww, I feel for him, my mum suffered awfully with her teeth. That was before people went to the dentist, so . . . I'd come back from school and she'd be on the sofa, a towel with a bag of ice on her face, mouth swelled all up. Knocked her down, nothing she could do. And he's like that, no painkillers.

—Why not painkillers?

Asked Jules.

—Recovery son, he doesn't take any drugs. Nothing strong.

—That's unfortunate.

—Yes, I feel for him too.

The pastor began:

—A famous theologian said that suffering, real suffering, is like being enslaved, and that being enslaved a man loses half his soul.

Neither Jules nor the woman knew how to react to that, so they didn't. He continued:

—But you say there's some progress, Jules? On the Gofundme?

He said this last as if with air quotes around it, as of one parading a new word and impressed with themselves to be doing so.

—Yeah, since last time anyway. Still not much, but it seems there's a bit of progress.

—That's great, isn't it? Never underestimate the kindness of people.

—It's true, it's the sort of thing makes you glad to be alive, no?

Jules shrugged.

—Hopefully soon enough we'll be able to get him booked up, get him sorted.

—You should tell him, tell him people care. He must be so lonely.

They looked up the room at the boots' soles.

—Ah, don't want to bother him like.

—No, he'll like it, it'll do him the world of good to know.

—It will.

Jules tarried a second, but could think of no excuse, and wandered up to the end of the room. At least he could speak without looking at him.

—Mal, mal.

He whispered very, very quietly.

—You awake? Don't if you're sleeping I'll . . .

—Yeah.

He made to sit up.

—No, don't, rest yourself, I heard you're not sleeping.

He made to sit up again.

—Have a wee rest, just want to tell you something. . . . Well it's basically, you remember that site I told you, the charity thing, to get started on the dentist's costs? It's really started to make some progress recently. We've got a good couple of hundred euro and I think we can expect more . . .

—Thank you.

—And Rupert was talking maybe get a collection going . . .

— . . .

—It's great like. All these people chipping in, really makes a difference.

— . . .

Jules had no idea what the silence meant: did he feel awkward, overwhelmed, too sore to care?

—Who is it's donating?

—It's my . . . friends. And some people they know.

—How come all these people are helping me?

—Well, like see that's the thing, it's almost like they're not doing anything. Just a bunch of people doing a small amount, like it's almost, think about it this way, if one million people were to give . . . a tenth of a cent, that would be your money got. So it's almost like they're not helping, you know? It's kind of inconsequent . . . meaningless to them, but it adds up.

—So there's lots of people?

—Who contributed?

—Aye.

—Well, yeah, kind of . . . maybe not, but it's still the same principle, I think . . . anyway what does it matter, the money will hopefully continue to come and we'll be sorted.

And now Mal did rise in earnest, looking more haggard than normal, and Jules stood up and told him, more or less truthfully, he had to leave, and left.

And despite this last awkwardness, he felt good. Better than good, in fact: out on the street, the cold winter air freshening his lungs, he felt something close to euphoria. The day seemed sharp and clear: its final cold sun on the wet shining streets, the sun's glints on bonnets and windscreens and the sunglasses of Italian tourists; teens in uniforms flirting noisily, waiting for buses, expanding to fill the space around them, and police watching suspiciously the sick-looking people with coke bottles containing clear liquid or water bottles with amber.

It signalled order. He felt as if he knew the order, that he'd opened up the back of life and peered into the wires. Each moment, each colour and each deed, that was where life was.

In the imperceptible nudges toward good and bad that is each moment, the chance to live well or badly.

And his role in that cosmos was clear—he was the one standing outside it, getting goodness started, instituting rather than following the rules. He's setting the people on the path to good, on their natural path, and once he has done so, once he has made these little alterations in the course of the men's lives, which will make up a big alteration in the course of Mal's life, he will stop, his job done, a little hero, a social engineer. Like Raskolnikov or Christ.

* * *

— . . . .

Jules stood in the softly lit living room of his father's house, looking at the partially opened envelope on the coffee table. The TV was on, in the corner, muted. His father wasn't in the room: Jules's silence was the silence of the perplexed, a silence which needs no interlocutor.

Or rather, it was the silence of one desperately trying to think of an excuse. He walked over to check that it was what he thought it was. He winced to see it confirmed. He had placed the order just two days ago, and had not expected it this early and so had left the house this morning before the mail came. He didn't know why his father had opened his mail, until he looked at the front of the envelope and saw that it didn't have a name, just an address, and he duly remembered that he hadn't put in a name, with a view to some sort of plausible deniability.

This opened up a possibility for him, just as he heard his father descending the stairs.

—What the hell is this?

He asked, brow fiercely creased. His father looked relaxed and unwontedly amused in baggy pajamas, evidently having just bathed.

—Came this morning.

—What is it?

—You tell me. It appears to be knickers.

—Knickers?

—Knickers.

Jules figured attack was the best form of defence.

—Why are you buying woman's knickers?

But his dad was waiting:

—Who said they were woman's? And who said they were bought?

— . . . knickers are by definition woman's. Can't have man's knickers. And as for buying, fine, why are you coming to acquire knickers?

—You tell me.

His father remained amused, and Jules felt himself reddening. And embarrassment morphed into irritation when he realized he really needed those fecking women's knickers.

It was his first customer, derrytogalai, who was causing the problems. He had asked Jules about the other, more biologically tricky, products currently out of stock, and Jules, in the market for a bit of repeat business, put him off and said that they'd be ready soon.

But derrytogalai kept asking. He thought about saying that he took the pill which suppressed periods for him, but he realised that that wouldn't work in this case, as he'd already said they would be available.

He became incredibly paranoid. He interpreted derrytogalai's innocent enough questions as indicating scepticism about whether he was what he claimed to be, and thought he was going to get found out. He toyed with closing his account. He'd had a reasonable run, after all, maybe it was time to give up.

But he was doing so well: by his reckoning, he had contributed at least €220 to the Gofundme (admittedly that was mostly from one customer who went massively beyond the call of duty, seemingly from a genuine desire to help), not to mention the knock-on effect in his customer's lives he was sure was happening.

So he did the only sensible thing: he made another account on the website, this time for buyers, planning to buy the requisite goods, and then send them on to derrytogalai. Of course, this would completely fuck with his own finances, but provided it didn't happen too frequently, he would just take that hit.

He realised, though, that it's at least possible that other vendors, like him, would use the same type of underwear for all their orders, and that imperilled things twice over: first, he may send someone underwear which the buyer recognised as belonging to another vendor. Or, on the other hand, he may send someone underwear which the buyer recognised as not belonging to him, carryon.

But that, it turns out, was no real obstacle. He contacted the cheapest seller he could find (he wasn't quite sure how the difference in price worked here; he suspected it was perhaps one of the clearest manifestations of the arbitrariness of pricing) and asked if he could get period underwear that was in the style attached, and he then sent a photo taken from Amazon of his brand.

The person duly agreed, for just a nominal extra fee, and so carryon got back to derrytogalai and told him that there's now that in stock, and he had planned to post them as soon as they arrived. But now that was in trouble.

—Well, chuck 'em out will you! You kept them on the table? Obviously some mistake. Which of us was it addressed to? Also, what's for dinner?

He watched his father, without responding, take the package out to the garden and thence, presumably, to the bin. He thought, glumly, about retrieving it from the rubbish.

10

— . . . and Christianity is all about second chances. It's the second chance we have of life in Christ, no matter what our background, what we've done. It's a message for *all* of us. And that's what we're celebrating today, and indeed what, in one way or another, we celebrate every week. But especially today . . . maybe some of you have been wondering why this man here . . .

Here he pointed to Malcolm, who was sitting on the raised part of the room beside him, in a suit and his hair combed and either gelled or wet.

—. . . is up here, whom you all, of course, know. And the reason is to celebrate his new life with him, a new life that all of you, who have given your time and money, and even beyond this room, people who have never met him before, have given. I won't pretend to understand it. As anyone who has received a text message from me can testify, I am not the most technologically adept.

There was a lot of polite quiet laughter.

—But there is, from what Jules tells me, a community out there, not rich people, but just people who want to help, and they reached out, and together, little by little they helped out . . . and I'm going to stop talking shortly—I promise!—but I want to just say the voice is such a powerful sign of regeneration, of the new life. One thinks of John the Baptist, the voice calling in the wilderness, announcing the new.

Mal pulled a face, widening his eyes, and provoked laughter. With mirth, the pastor continued:

—Big shoes to fill, yes? But anyway, to celebrate the new voice . . . he's just out from the dentist on Friday and still in some pain, he tells me . . . but soon, eh, it will be over . . . but to celebrate with him, Malcolm, and his new voice, wants to say a couple of words.

He stood up, a piece of paper in his hand, and shuffled to the dais. Wiping a clot of greying hair from his brow he began:

—This is kind of . . . in at the deep end for me as Rupert says new voice . . . . I won't keep you . . . Thanks to everybody . . . but especially thanks to Jules. For a perfect stranger here because the social are forcing him, to do this for me, to set all this up, it's magic to me, like, but thanks, son.

Some people applauded Jules. Sara, who had been avoiding the church but was today in the audience, turned to him and smiled wistfully.

—Some of you know my story, some not. I won't go on about it too much. It's one you've all heard. Bruiser father, terrified mother, no family life, left school. Then drank. That's it, really. Quick, right?

The pastor smiled, the audience laughed warmly.

—My friend, my best friend died in the same room as me, and I came here, after a quick six months in hospital. But even then I couldn't speak about it . . . the teeth. Now I can. And now I want to give something back, to try to give others a second chance the way I have been given one.

Again some spontaneous applause. People were really very happy.

—And it's all about family. That's the most important thing for us. Family. That's what we need, that's where we've gone wrong!

A couple of smatterings of applause, a 'Go on Mal!', a sea of smiling faces.

—Family has been eroded. Fathers aren't fathers, and the women today aren't women. I see them, barely grown, in their heels with their naggins, making spectacles of themselves, puking their guts up in Temple Bar, getting pregnant and getting abortions and getting . . .

He lost himself a bit in his rhetoric and paused. A sort of emotional inertia meant that most people's faces hadn't caught up to the turn in his speech, and remained smiling, if a bit blankly and gluely so. Jules winced. Rupert frowned.

—And the men, what can they do? If women are now men, where do they have to go? They've been pushed out, 'man' is a bad word . . . and so we see it . . .

There was some hope that maybe things were righting themselves. Mal paused for dramatic effect, and thudded down, with righteous anger:

—the family destroyed. . . and we wonder, we bring our kids up, and we wonder why they turn to drugs and worse. No role models, no hope, no men, no women, no family. Well I am going to fight, for us, the people sitting by O'Connell, going to fight for the Irish family for all of us! And an . . .

And thinking this was as good a moment as any to break into things the pastor rose and started clapping loudly, imprecating the first row to do so, and then applause filled the room, and the pastor and Mal shook hands and exchanged words off mic. Jules, who had barely slept all night and was feeling dark, sneaked up and headed for the door, the thought of post-service tea and biscuits and apple juice with the newly voiced Mal too much to bear.

He was thinking of Carrie. On returning from New Orleans he had told himself that the whole thing was her fault, that she should have tried to reach out more, or something like that. At least, he had felt zero empathy for her, hadn't considered how *she* felt. He had enough to do thinking about himself, about his injuries, and then finals, and then Sara and JobPath . . . it had just got lost. Last night though, that changed. Last night little thoughts came to him: how she had hugged him outside the cemetery even though he'd been quiet and morose and making little effort; how he'd woken up in the middle of the night and felt the bed shaking, and knew she was crying but made no effort, pretended to still be asleep. He had thought, then, of nothing but his own pain. Now he felt hers. That mere empathy brought her closer, and he found himself thinking of her positive qualities, of the undeniable good times. But those thoughts were all hugely painful. And they were so because of what spurred them: a naked picture of Carrie, which derrytogalai had sent him.

He had been unable to retrieve the underwear which had been put in the bin, which he had intended to send to derrytogalai. His father, through accident or design, had disposed of a stew in the bin shortly afterward, and the only way to salvage them would have been to wash them, which would obviously defeat the purpose. He thought first to place another order, and go through the whole procedure again. But that would be both expensive and a hassle, and he was more than a little worried about the same sort of thing happening again. And he next thought of just giving up, running away and cutting his losses, content to have made some small difference in the world. But it was just this, that he had been making some small difference in the world, that made him reticent. He had just the day before reached the preliminary goal of the Gofundme, and the site suggested he add a secondary stretch goal, and he had done so. He didn't want to give it up.

He found himself, again, regretting that he wasn't a woman. If he were, he could placate him with a Skype call or something. But then he had an idea. He had plenty of naked pictures of Carrie, from the long eight months after she had left Dublin but before he had come to New Orleans. He thought maybe he could send one or two to derrytogalai: ones that didn't so much show her face, and which weren't thus traceable back to her in any way. That, after all, would be a victimless crime.

He had, in fact, in his head, the perfect pictures to use: one taken looking down at her naked body, and one which she had somehow taken on a timer of her whole body, and which didn't include her face. Pleased with his plan — no one would get hurt, and Mal would benefit — he resolved to do it when he got home, and later that day found the pictures on his computer. He had misremembered one of them—there was a bit of her face in the top corner, although nowhere near enough to identify her. He scrupled a little, still, about whether this was crossing a line. But not for long. He did it and, having arranged the trade with derrytogalai, sent the pictures. And then he had thought the problem had gone away, and his scheme was going to live to see another day, until he woke one morning to find in his inbox the 'tribute' from derrytogalai: a printout of one of the pictures, on which he had masturbated.

Almost instantly, on seeing it, he came to regret everything: not just the photo, but the whole plan that had led up to it. The sense that he'd had, that he was a microscopic force for good in the world now was gone, the self-satisfaction replaced with queasiness. And so it was with some very dark thoughts he walked from the church back across the Liffey, regretting the last months, Malcolm's rant repeating in his head.

* * *

—So . . . are you just not going to say anything?

—Are you not?

—Dude. You know how much I was looking forward to it. I'm crushed.

—Me too.

— . . . —Are you just going to parrot back what I say?

—No.

—You're such a fucking emotionless person.

That, eight months ago, was the last conversation he had had with Carrie. A couple of days after he received the picture he continued the thread:

—Hey. How's it going?

He then waited for hours until Carrie got up, nothing to do, traipsing the streets around Trinity waiting for her reply, which came mid-afternoon:

—He lives.

—Yeah, just about. How's things?

—Eh, been better.

—How so?

—Long story.

—Ah.

A pause. Jules was inattentively skimming the cheap maths paperbacks in Hogges Figgis.

—You?

—Yeah not too bad, interesting.

—Yeah?

—Yeah, been doing stuff like the charity work a bit.

—Good deal.

A pause.

—Look, I just want to say I'm really, really sorry.

—Okkaaayy . . . —for what precisely?

—Everything.

A pause

—For being a dick in the conversation above.

—Ah. —I see. —Why now! —*?

—Just. Wanted to say. I regret it.

—Why did you not talk to me?

—Well, what could we do? We're so far apart.

—And you just realized that?? You've known from the beginning . . . like why would you even get in a relationship with somebody so far from you? Who was gonna leave the country?

—Because I liked you.

—And then you stopped?

—No. But what else could we do? —Where could we go after NOLA?

—Fought for it for Christ's sake, shown some . . . something.

—But just to stop like that, it's like you didn't give a fuck.

—My mouth was killing me! I really don't think you get it.

—I get it. I know. That trip was a disaster. But that's it? —A bad visit and that's it? You know I would have come over. You know I was going to. —Like, if that's all it took, then I repeat, why start a relationship with someone who you didn't have strong feelings for? And then keep it up for months and months and months. —Were you regretting it the whole time, humoring me?

—Nooo. Those were for real some of the happiest times in my life.

—But then? —Did you just want an Internet girlfriend or something? A pen pal?

—No.

—Then what?

—I don't know. I didn't think.

—Think about what?

—You, us, I just thought, I came all this way and now I'm fucked, I've got to find loads of money, we're not going to see each other for ages, and even then, what?

—I know, it was a disaster. But like, in a certain sense, so? Disasters happen, right?

—Yeah. It was just shitty, and I didn't know what to do. Still don't. Just wanted to say, I'm sorry.

—Right. —Well, whatever. —So I guess. —You maybe need to think of other people more.

Carrie paused.

—I do, I'm really trying to. I didn't get it, like how you felt. But now I do. And I'm sorry. That's all I really want to say. I should have done things better.

—Okay, well, I gtg right now. —But thanks, I think.

—Thanks for listening. I really am very sorry for any hurt I caused you. That's not what I wanted.

—Okay, well, thanks I guess.

11

Zach pointed to his full beer:

—I just got this, let me finish it. You were gone forever.

—Yeah sorry, Jordan was having a thing.

—Oh, yeah?

—Yeah it's nothing.

—Got your charger?

—Yeah, actually no, but doesn't matter, c'mon let's goooo already.

He raised his eyebrows. She smiled.

—Okay, gimme a sec, let me get an uber.

His hand reached for his pocket.

—No! You drink your beer, I'll order the uber.

—But you don't know my address.

—Well, it's a good job there's a way of transferring information from person to person isn't there?

—Bluetooth?

—Tell me your address dude . . . you sure you need that beer? Don't want you falling asleep on me.

It's safe to say Carrie had no fucking clue what she was doing. Once Jordan had left, she had planned to switch her phone off and ignore Zach who anyway, she was sure, was very soon going to want to ignore her. But she just couldn't bear to be alone in the house that night, thinking about what had happened, and anyway she had no booze, and the bar would be the only place open, so she just went back and hoped that maybe he'd not find out, and then she could, in time, tell her side of the story. I mean, it was weird, yeah, but it didn't make her a bad person, right? He'd see that. But it was best to wait a bit: not tonight. So she wanted to make sure he didn't learn things already from a prejudicial source, at least not until he'd got to know her a bit better. Thankfully, he seemed amenable: he downed his beer and told her the address and they settled up and went outside to wait for the car which drove them to his place.

* * *

Half teasingly, smiling, but annoyed, she asked:

—Come onnnnn, what are you, gay?

—I mean . . .

Here he gestured to his naked bottom half, which suggested he wasn't. He was still wearing his shirt on his top. It was a strange ensemble.

—I just wanna check my phone real quick and then . . .

—Man. I'm. Right. Here.

She scootched off the bed and went and kissed him and started stroking his cock.

—Jeez, you're not shy.

—You are correct, sir.

He kissed her back and they fell on the bed, but soon he was off it again.

—???

—Condom.

—Okay, well be quick already.

He went back to his pants.

—Oh, kept a condom in your pants did you? Confident?

And the phone was out and . . .

—Aw man, you're obsessed dude.

He was checking it. He frowned, put the phone down, put the condom on, and got back on the bed.

—So, uh, any interesting news?

—Oh, I've got interesting news.

Somehow he'd misunderstood that as somewhat abstract dirty talk and was continuing.

—Hah, I mean with your phone.

—What?

—Nothing, good.

And she pulled him closer to her.

— . . .

— . . .

—Hey, you heard from that guy Max recently? Jordan's friend?

Through somewhat laboured breath:

—What? —Now don't talk . . . about . . . Jor-dan.

Satisfied by his reaction, she relaxed a bit and turned her attention gladly to the task at hand.

A man and his phone, however, are not easily parted and after only acceding to her faked demands for a cuddley-kissy period afterward for a couple of minutes he got up and was again by his discarded pants. At this point she just thought fuck it.

—Oh shit, man!

—What?

—My friend's having a meltdown on Facebook!

—Max?

—What is your obsession with Max? You know he's gay, right?

—Nothing, not obsessed, nothing.

—It's crazy, he's been in this fight with his roommates because they took the quarters he saved for the washer and replaced them with bills, as if they didn't know, and anyway they got in a big fight, and he just came back after being out and found that they'd like passive-aggressively washed everything he owns, and obviously like he got super pissed at that, coz they went through all this shit . . . he says he's gonna call the cops but like my friend commented what're you gonna say, he washed all my shit? That's crazy man.

—That's it?

—What? You don't think that's crazy?

—Yeah, it's crazy.

Whether through a combination of a post-coital tristesse, or all her weird questions, Zach was beginning to get a bit wary of Carrie.

—But come on here, don't just pump and dump me dude, lie with me. You millennials and your social media . . .

—You're two years younger than me!

—But have I looked at my phone once? See I live in the moment. Live in the moment with me.

They lived in the moment, and then slept in the moment, but when Carrie woke up at 8am he was already awake, and the first syllable told her that he knew.

—So Max was in touch.

—Oh, yeah?

—Yeah.

—Cool.

She lay back down on her side, pretending to rest. She still had no clue what the fuck she was doing. And with the alcohol gone from her system, her assessment of how readily she'd be able to explain everything to Zach was lowered. She decided she wanted to get out.

—Said Jordan's living with him now?

—Oh yeah, he said something about that.

—Because of you?

—What?

—Because of you.

—That's weird.

A pause, and Carrie continued:

—Uh.

She got up, found her clothes.

—I better get going. Thanks for having me over.

—Uh . . . did you threaten Jordan?

—No, there was a mix-up, things got fucked up . . . on the Internet.

—Things got fucked up on the Internet?

—Yeah, like . . .

She was putting her socks on now, not looking at him.

—On the Internet, things got fucked up.

—Reversing the order of the words doesn't really make it any clearer.

—Yeah . . .

Shoes on.

— . . . anyway, I have a . . . bus to catch. Thanks again.

And she darted out the door, not looking at him, cringing and wondering where, precisely, she was.

* * *

On Christmas Day Carrie went to the emergency room. Things hadn't been going so well.

—Nah, yeah things have been going very well, thank you.

There was a sheen of sweat on her and she was pallid, sitting on a thin table, disturbed by the medical smell and the doctor's attention, and high and drunk. She spoke quickly.

—Just this chest infection's all, is all, it's something I've suffered from them for many years, nothing new.

—And how long have you had it?

—Oh, few days, I mean, or so, just last night—of all nights—I didn't really sleep so good because of breathing, and then this afternoon it got a bit worse.

—And . . . so you've been drinking?

—Yeah well, it's Christmas, doctor.

—And, anything else?

—Nah, nah.

—You seem a bit agitated.

—Ah, yeah.

—Yeah?

—Well, see I have an exam coming up, and I have ADHD, so I had to do some studying this morning before the festivities, so I took an Adderall, always makes me like this.

And she made something in the vicinity of somber jazz hands, attempting to gesture at her body.

—You know you shouldn't drink and take Adderall at the same time, right? That can be dangerous because you drink too much without realizing.

—Yeah, yeah I don't, normally, just these are extraneous circumstances. It's really just my chest, I'm fine otherwise . . . you know clarithromycin? That's what I normally take.

—Okay, well, just let me see.

—Ex*tenu*ating . . .

—What?

—Nothing.

—Your heart's beating quickly.

—Yeah.

—How much Adderall did you take?

—Just the normal.

He looked at her; she reddened.

—This is too quick. It's dangerous. Are you sure?

—I'm sure, it's really just my chest.

—And . . . you know you shouldn't smoke with a chest infection? If you've had them before, you know this, right?

—Yeah I know, I didn't smoke today.

He looked at her; she reddened.

— . . . I did yesterday, didn't know it was bad, thought I could just fight it off, sometimes I do, I don't always get 'em see, haven't in fact last two years, thought I was over it.

She was starting to panic: even her truths sounded, even to her, like lies. He started to smile in a way that she found creepy, as if he was turning on a switch to become nice; it felt like pity.

—Okay, well, from what it sounds like I'm sure you're right, it's an infection . . . and I'll write a prescription for you . . . so you're with friends, family today?

—Yes.

—Which one?

—Yep.

—??

—Oh, friends, my roommate Jordan and I are having a quiet day. So thanks . . .

—And did he bring you here?

Her voice wavered, to her annoyance, as she said:

—No, came by myself . . . he's back at home waiting, he made the dinner.

Again, a look.

—Well, see the receptionist on the way out. You really can't drink or smoke or take Adderall on this, right?

—Trust me, I won't, I just want to rest and get better. So thanks.

She got her bag and left quickly, stopping off at a 24/7 drive-through pharmacy in a completely deserted mall, before returning to the apartment.

It was a mess, with a sack full of wine and beer bottles awkwardly by the door where her shoes go (it's meant to be in such an annoying place she'll take them out, but so far that hasn't happened), clothes strewn on the floor, a series of plates by the sink. Jordan's departure hadn't done great things to the place.

It hadn't done great things to Carrie, either. Since he left, indeed already that first day she got back from Zach's, she felt like she'd been travelling in some temporal dimension orthogonal to the past-future line, moving further and further away from the onwardly travelling mass of humanity which had been heading for Christmas.

She felt more invisible than ever: her classes ended, and so she had no cause to do work or to interact with people, even online. And it's not like anybody was there for her to interact with. Each morning she would wake up and come out to the living room, and it would be as it was before: no cereal bowl or smell of coffee, the TV not left on CNN as Jordan sometimes did, no smell of shower gel from the shower. Abandoned, it felt like.

She had never, actually, lived alone, even if sometimes it had felt like it: she went from her mom's to her grandparents' to always having roommates in college. And now doing so, at this time, she was unrestrained and her days quickly assumed a shape that was disturbing even to her. Waking up bleary and tense after little sleep, she would pulverize half an Adderall and sniff it to wake herself up, then do a few hours relatively unfocused work (she did power through a decent chunk of Shakespeare at this period, its only saving grace), pretty much waiting until dinnertime when she thought it acceptable to start drinking and temper the stimulant. As Christmas took over the TV and the stores played the old music and sold the old things, and as the days headed toward the solstice, she continued on her path, each day worse than the next, until finally she woke up barely able to breath.

Now she lay on the couch, the beginnings of a cumulative hangover announcing itself, feeling as if her invisibility had been broken in the worst possible way, thinking again and again of the suspicious and then pitying look of the doctor, feeling suspicious and then pitying of herself.

12

People Are Data: A New Feminist Myth?

Carrie Ann North

Donna Haraway's *A Cyborg Manifesto* posited that certain binaries which have long held sway in theorizing the person—such as that of natural vs. machine, human vs. animal, and physical vs. non-physical—had, in the late twentieth century, broken down. In their stead, she suggested, as 'ironic political myth', that the concept of cyborg, the neither (or both) artificial and natural should guide our theorizing.

Haraway was writing in 1984, in an age before the personal computer, when the Internet was still barely existent. A lot has changed since then, and a natural question to ask is what becomes of her myth when updated to take account of contemporary technology.

In this talk, I want to sketch an answer: that person as cyborg is to be replaced with person as data. I shall make the case for this by sketching the economic conception of personal identity: that what a person is—at least for many, at least from the early moderns on— is informed and determined by the economic paradigm which holds sway in the person's society. It's gone from machines to cyborgs or computers but now it is data. I'll show that data plays many of the roles traditionally attributed to the person, and how the framework can lead, in a Harawayian fashion, to a truly intersectional praxis of women, people of color, LGBTQ, and so on.

Carrie reread the abstract, for a conference in NYU in a couple of months, tense and weak but mind firing almost painfully quickly. She'd been entirely sober ten days: in the first couple she slept and felt miserable, but gradually disabling guilt left, and she felt herself beginning to recover, and a few days later her chest was no longer bothering her and she had energy again.

This was almost worse than being sick. The sudden enforced sobriety was a shock. It wasn't that she was, normally, a very heavy drinker or anything, but she came to realize that even drinking a couple of times a week played an important regulative function in her mind. With more hours of lucidity than she was used to, she stretched out into erstwhile overlooked corners of her mind, and these corners were uniformly bad. She had a lot of psychic pain that, when thus disturbed, got stirred up, and became part of the daily rhythm of her thinking. She would shudder at formerly repressed memories which now had conscious space to luxuriate, which would assail her from nowhere when she was showering, eating, on the cusp of sleep.

One of the main sources of shuddering was Jules. When he left New Orleans, she felt that he had wronged her: that the whole thing was his fault, or at least not hers. What she wanted, then, was a sign, some communication to show that he recognized this and was willing to fight for her.

But the sign wasn't forthcoming, and she came to think that his feelings couldn't have been that strong, and this hurt her, as she felt he was being callous. Hurt, in turn, morphed into anger at just how *rude* he was being, and that proved to be the emotional sticking point. Fuck that guy, she thought, reducing the complexity of her feelings to that sentiment, and trying to go about her life. That—the start of a new term, the new course, the failed tinder attempts, Jordan—hadn't succeeded in changing her feelings.

Now, though, she was in a new psychic place. Now she looked forward hopelessly and back with regret and self-hatred. She started thinking back, despite herself, fondly to their time together: she couldn't help thinking that it was two winters ago she was in Dublin, happier than she'd ever been, as she woke each day to an empty apartment and a quiet phone. She started seeing him in her mind's eye, and, despite the anger, just wanting his presence in her life. But she knew it was hopeless: the past was over and it was very clear they had no future.

Her response was to try to drown out this hopelessness in work. Once she had regained her strength, she found a lucidity she'd almost never encountered before, and threw herself into her research about the nature of identity.

It was tough going at first. She had moved on from the early moderns to consider recent work that considers human beings as computers, from Turing on to a lot of work in contemporary 'analytic' philosophy. After all, if personal identity is determined by what drives the economy, then, she thought, personal identity should be thought of as computational, since computers are what drives the economy.

But she struggled to make sense of this: she read about rooms with monoglot English speakers manipulating pieces of card with Chinese characters, and of zombies, but it got submerged under numbered premises and dry prose. And it just didn't *feel* right, to her: she linked the thought in her head with logic, and if there was one thing she knew about life, it was that it isn't logical.

One day around New Year, reading, for some reason, about Gödel's incompleteness theorems, she decided to take the day off. It was still early, though, and there was nothing to do, and she was facing up to many hours of consciousness with just the TV for distraction, when she read an article about pantact.

She had, since hearing about it at the party, instinctively stayed away from it: she thought her past could be divided into happy moments, reliving which would make her wistful, and sad ones which would make her sad. But curiosity and emptiness got the better of her that afternoon, and she tentatively loaded it up. She had got the account when she first heard about it (there is a registration period required, in which the app makes requests for your data from the various companies), but had never used it; now she did, picking, anxiously, a date around the start of the academic term that she imagined would be pretty emotionally untroubling.

Almost immediately she saw why everyone was so nuts about this app: it was really very fun. She was immediately drawn back to that fall: there had been a scandal involving an LA state senator that had made the big news, and it was super amusing to her and her Facebook friends—she enjoyed reading the old jokes and the stories about it. It created a very odd sense of distortion: of seeing something that now means absolutely nothing occupying a significant portion of your (past) attention. And she read, with amusement, the messages from Charlie, her poor-quality tinder date, in a new light. She had been, for some reason, extremely confident that when he replied to her flirtatious, jokey messages dourly it was because he was not one for wasting time on text messages; she attributed a presence to him on the basis of this which he really did not have.

She relived a few of those days from the fall and the end of the summer before it, with a wincing tension in the back of her head but nevertheless fascination, and as the evening drew on she decided to take a risk and plunge further back, to her fourteenth birthday which she remembered as an unambiguously pleasant time. That was even more uncanny, the interfaces on the webpages looking all old, reading her toe curlingly earnest posts on Facebook about PETA and reading texts from her first boyfriend, again noticing that she imputed to his lack of gorm a strength behind the silence which in retrospect—he was fourteen, after all—wasn't there. But most stirring was a text conversation she had had with her mom about what her birthday dinner was going to be, laughing anew at her inability to text abbreviate properly, her thinking that 'wuw 4 dins' is an acceptable way to ask what you wanted for dinner. Although it was definitely bittersweet, still there was a sweetness to it, and when she closed the app a few hours later, she felt emotionally satisfied as she hadn't for a while.

What was most impressive to her, and what made her realize why it was so popular, was the feeling it gave you. It really did feel like being transported back in time, the sort of sense you get, fleetingly, through snippets of music or biscuits in French novels.

She was just brushing her teeth, walking around her living room as she did so, when a thought hit her powerfully. Keeping the toothbrush in her mouth, she went to the computer and opened a document:

pantact stores experiences

pantact stores data

experiences are data

people are experiences

And a rush of euphoria hit her as she realized what five was, then she typed triumphantly:

people are data!!!!!!!!!!!!!!!!!

She stared at the screen for a long time, mouth salival and minty fresh, and then went to bed and didn't sleep until it was almost light. It made perfect sense: it was data, now, that drove the economy (or at least it would once someone learned how to monetize it properly), not computers, and it made sense of the fact that people seem to live so much of their lives online now. And that a person was just the sum of their experiences, also, seemed reasonable, and was hardly an outlier view in the theory of personal identity. Deeper than that, though, it just *felt* right, too, and once she had worn her mind out with thinking she drifted off to sleep feeling that the world was more intelligible to her than it had been for a very long time.

13

It's unclear who the first people to interpersonate were, but you could probably find, with a little googling, the first think piece to say it was creepy as fuck. Interpersonation was basically giving control of one's pantact to another, and granting them full access to all your data. It was viewed, by its users, as the ultimate commitment, a way of really truly giving yourself to another, of maybe even something more, of becoming one with them.

Loads of people were creeped out by it, talking of how it was simply another iteration of our damaging need to share everything about ourselves online, how privacy was a good thing, and so on. And there was plenty of concern about the security implications: the thought that mayyyybe it's not such a great idea for infatuated fifteen-year-olds to be giving over all their personal information to someone they barely knew. None of the stuff she read, though, seemed to realize what Carrie did, that it was making possible the sort of union with another person previously found only among mystics or mythmakers.

She set about writing a piece about interpersonation, using it as a springboard to introduce her theory of People As Data, and as the spring term came around she felt herself happier than ever, completely losing herself in work she thought was good and important.

And, despite herself, there was another reason: it was around then that Jules made contact again. Initially his first message had, when she woke that morning, simply enervated her more, recalling instantly the bitterness that she had long choked down. But as the days passed, and the sense repeated on her that he really did feel bad about it, she came to see things differently. Merely that he tried, that some human reached out to her, meant an awful lot right then, after the sober mania and the binge, and

Jordan . . .

She wanted to stay mad: found herself thinking of arguments and snark, questions she wanted answered, and so on. She didn't want, out of self-respect, to let him back in just like that. But the desire for self-respect was trumped by the greater desire simply to have someone she formerly cared deeply about in her life, even if just as a 5,000 miles away friend.

The first week or so was tentative: a text here and there, feeling each other out, excessively polite and serious, exchanging (heavily redacted) information about the period they hadn't been in touch. She having trouble with her roommate; he selling all his shit on eBay for spare cash. But after a certain point she found he was occupying more of her thoughts, and she thought, perhaps, that the same was happening for him: they somehow fell back into the habit of talking every day, and she came to realize that she liked, again, waking up to texts from him, hearing his dispatches from the dark Dublin she remembered, the one always set six hours ahead of her.

Soon they were sharing details of their lives as they had before. Carrie found loads of funny photos in her camera roll she had collected and had had no one to share with, and started unloading them, at first making a slight pretence that, look, I was at the store today and found this tres leche with 'std' written on it, but after a while she just started straight up sending funny photos, happy to see his uncharacteristically amused response with too many 'ha's': 'hahaha'.

And he did the same: when a little sparrow, or something like that, flew in his bedroom window and wouldn't get out he managed to take some video and whatsapp her it, and she in return said, 'that's AMAZING' which, while it was pretty good, it wasn't.

Carrie didn't really know what it meant, and in fact was happy to think that it didn't mean anything, that it was just desired communication, but she liked the extra 'ha's' or the capitals, the sense that they were trying to impress each other, were acting as they would to a potential romantic partner.

She came to think back to Dublin, increasingly, with fondness. To that winter and spring in Dublin: with the wind colder than any she, a lifelong southern girl, had ever known, with walking across the small, beautiful Trinity campus as darkness fell at dinnertime, lights shining in the arts block and the differing Irish accents which she prided herself, completely baselessly, on being able to discriminate, walking from the library where she'd been reading Butler or about four dimensionalism, the view that we are extended in space as in time, or Tom Paulin's translation of *Antigone*.

She'd leave then and walk around silent, dark New Square, looking up at the window of Jules's lovely apartment, enjoying the cold night air, looking out beyond the cricket pitch at Nassau Street, light and alive.

Then she would go up, finding the door expressly open, saying, 'knock, knock' and going to his bedroom, and he'd be there, facing away from the door by the window dark now, in front of his computer, and she'd put her arms on him and he'd turn round and they'd kiss and one or both would cook while one or both read or they chatted or something else. It only really occurred to her now, the memory of her relationship with him having been overshadowed by the bad events, that this was perhaps the clearest case of happiness she knew, and it was confusing because she didn't think such happiness was meant for her, but her stomach burned for it, to be back then and there, and that impelled her, as it had done before, to keep the text conversation going, pointless, as it seemed to her, as it would inevitably be. Even though there's nothing to be done and it just makes no sense, conceptually, to start dating someone 5,000 miles away, it doesn't stop her reaching out.

* * *

—Well, ah, that's interesting.

—You think it's bullshit?

—It sounds very Butlerian.

Carrie laughed, or rather expelled air through her nose.

—Oh, man! Is there any worse insult, coming from you?

Carrie and Jules were skyping. The first two or three times they did it had somehow been so entirely effortless that they expected it would always henceforth be effortless. But there was something awkward and stilted about their conversation today, and that made Carrie start blabbing about her theory.

—So people are data.

—Yeah dude, hence the name of the theory, 'People Are Data'.

—You named your theory? Like a pet?

—Like a baby more like.

—But like, data is inert.

—Inert?

—Yeah, it doesn't do anything. It can't see things, it can't taste pineapple.

—So?

—People can see things, people can taste pineapple. So people aren't data.

—Ah my man, that's the interactivity objection, that's what I call it.

—Oh, you've thought of this?

—Shit yeah. And basically the reply is fuck interactivity.

And here Jules laughed.

—Well, I guess that makes philosophy pretty easy if you can just say, 'fuck blah', for every problem with your theory.

—You really think people care that much about interactivity? I bet you have one of those Facebook friends who posts a shit ton and no one ever interacts with, right? Or even think of that one friend who just always fucking *talks*, do you think they care?

—Hmm, I guess I know someone like that.

—We all do, it's a thing. And like, I think I can even make sense of interactivity, too. For me, interactivity is just a sort of infiniteness, like if you can always keep on learning about someone, that's enough, you can sort of travel forward in life with them and they're always new. And you can do that with pantact: you travel forward by going sequentially through their data, their days. Admittedly, you belong to different times, but so? We belong to different spaces and that doesn't matter. Like, what is this interaction? We're just transferring info, learning new stuff about each other. That's enough I think.

—But what about like . . .

—Fucking?

—Well, I wouldn't have put it quite so . . .

—Nah wait a sec, you don't let me finish.

—Okay.

—So you can, for most people, keep on going forward, at least for like decades, you can live with them, by just going through their past. You go forward in time going back in time with them. Or forward in time if you start their pantact at the start.

—Yeah, but they're not like *with* you, right? There's not another person there. It's just you, alone, with a bunch of zeros and ones.

—I don't know dude, I think I'd say it's always just you alone, whether there's also a bunch of zeros and ones there or a sentient bag of meat, I don't really think there's that much of a diff. If you're constantly receiving new information about the person, they're there.

—Well, you've reassured me, I was wondering if you didn't really appreciate the bodiness . . .

—Nah man, trust me, I appreciate the meat bags for sure.

—Do you though?

—Oh I appreciate. Bodies are overrated.

—Yeah?

—Yeah.

—Yeah.

Then there was a strange silence, as both were thinking, and were thinking that the other was thinking, simultaneously of the violence which had separated them, and the sex which had come before it. The latter thought won the day, and they both noted it.

—What?

—What yourself.

—Do you never get tired of being a parrot?

And she made a sort of squawking noise that sounded pretty accurate.

—That's a good squawk you got.

There was a pause.

—I'm horny, dude.

—Me, too.

—Yeah? Prove it.

—Help me prove it?

—Yeah?

—Please.

—So, ah, maybe close your eyes there a sec.

He did, and when he opened them was greeted with her shirtless, the same sun lighting her now uncovered shoulders. Jules:

—Uh, close your eyes a second.

She did, and when she opened them was faced with an artlessly close-up patch of shade.

—It's all black!

He bent over in order to see the picture-in-picture of his own camera, trying to work out its line of sight better, and readjusted himself and then managed to get his dick into the shot.

—Uh, this is not good, wait.

He took the laptop and placed it on the end of his lap and tilted the screen down, and a patch of white skin came in to view. Carrie said, still sort of light of tone:

—You weren't joking about being horny.

But Jules, with more seriousness and earnestness:

—You look good.

—Why, thank you.

Again in the same sort of flirtatious tone, but it sort of fell flat, felt half-hearted, and then there was silence apart from scratches of hand on jeans or breathing, and they watched each other, and when they'd finished Jules said *welllll* and Carrie laughed. And that broke but also sort of created a cordon round the silence, as if it were something set apart.

14

—But I just don't get why.

—I know, I know. I don't really either.

Jordan was talking to Carrie in a Starbucks by a highway.

—I feel like it just revealed this really dark side of you.

—Yeah, I'm sorry. I mean, I could blame all this shit on . . . I don't know, but I'm not gonna. It was a super weird thing to do. But really, nothing came of it, right? They never did anything. You didn't hear from them again?

—Well, no. But it caused problems. I had to go home. And I ended up telling my mom what happened. And that, well.

—Not good?

—She, I could tell, it just sort of confirmed her idea, like that it was my fault or something. She said something like 'well if you do *things like that*'.

—Awww fuck. Like really, if I would have known . . . Anyway, I get everything of your reaction. But you will come back? I promise, well I would say it's never going to happen again but that's ridiculous. Just come back.

—I will come back. I mean, I have nowhere else to go.

—Well that's great, your stuckness is my gain.

He didn't really laugh at this attempt at humour. But it was enough that he was coming back. She figured she'd be in the doghouse for a while but would soon be able to win him round: she guessed his nature was fundamentally a forgiving one, and in this she was right.

Things continued to look up for Carrie. As the term started again, she had written a short piece about personal identity and interpersonation, arguing that according to the Lockean view personal identity is determined by memories, and that one could think of interpersonation as a couple coming to share memories and thus selves, and that the clearest way to understand this was to hold that the self was data.

People had, it seems, received it very well: she had put it on medium.com and it got an awful lot of views from people agreeing or disagreeing, and she'd got a couple of informal emails from people asking her to speak at stuff.

Jules was coming to be a problem for her psychic balance, though. She felt reignited in her the feelings she had for him. But this caused sadness: they were so distant, and that distance seemed unbridgeable: neither had money to cross the Atlantic. It was just conceptually bad to try and be together, when they would have so few chances actually to be together in person.

She remained in the coffee shop after Jordan was gone, doing some work. She was giving a lecture at the faculty seminar in a couple of weeks—her first one, set up by her supervisor whom she had told about her essay—and was going to do a low-pressure test run. But she was thinking more about Jules, and texted him:

—Listen, I've been feeling anxious about this whole situation of ours again. . . . —I think I'm coming to feel for you strongly again, and after last time, I don't want to.

—I see. I've been feeling the same. But I don't, like even if I don't want things to get fucked up, I DEFINITELY don't want you not to be in my life anymore . . . if I compare now to two months ago, now is definitely better.

—I agree, but what can we do?

—I know.

—Like, realistically . . . —I'm not gonna be able to get over there.

—No, nor me there . . . —Until I get a fucking job.

—Right.

—Acckk why does life have to be so complicated?

—Well, I guess we can just continue.

—Continue?

—Yeah, like just what we're doing. If you want to?

—I don't know. I feel after last time we can't just leave things, you know?

—What mean?

—Well, it's coming up two years since we saw each other non-disastrously.

—lol —Yeah :/

—I feel it hanging over me. Makes me anxious.

—I know what you mean.

—Well look, I can and will really try.

—Try what?

—I don't know, find work, get money. We're looking at what, 500 plus spending money-ish?

—Yeah, like 800 dollars to here from Dublin, I looked.

—Right.

—That's not impossible.

—So we just wait?

—I guess we just wait.

—I can't wait.

—I don't know what else to say.

The conversation made her feel no better whatsoever, and she turned her phone over and tried to work.

* * *

—Eh right, okay, so I'm gonna bait and switch, gonna start talking about this cool new technology stuff and then when you're interested, going to go on about seventeenth-century British empiricism for a bit. So fair warning . . . And also, this is a test run of a talk I gotta give next week in front of frankly more important people than you.

She paused for laughter, and they duly laughed.

—So I'm gonna do it scholarly, sorry if it's maybe a bit tedious . . . but hey, I'm not going to read it at least.

Carrie looked to the back of the room where around fifteen

people were sitting, and her tone shifted to that of one reading words printed on their mind:

—I'm sure you've all heard of interpersonation, but if not first I'll introduce it and then try to convince you that theorists, and particularly those of us concerned with queer theory or feminism broadly construed, can learn some interesting lessons from it.

Interpersonation is a feature of the app pantact, an app which lets the user, as they market it, 'time travel' by replaying, for a given day, all of the user's Internet interactions. To interpersonate is to give control of one's pantact over to one's romantic partner—I don't know actually if there's non-romantic examples?—normally as a sign of commitment.

The argument I want to make is that in so doing one is literally—and I mean that literally literally—merging oneself with another, and that therefore modern technology allows people modalities of being hitherto consigned to mystic or religious experiences (think Plato's *Symposium*, or Tantric sex, or Christian mystics).

My argument has two steps. First, I argue, following John Locke, that two people sharing a sufficient number of the same experiences should count as the same person. The second is the explanatory claim of why this should be: here, drawing on the work of Judith Butler, I argue that the overlap of memory suffices for two people to be the same because people just are memory, or, more particularly, because they are the data memory encodes. People are data, and since pantact stores the same data as memory, pantact captures a person just as well as a brain does. So sharing a pantact is like sharing a brain. The overall conclusion is that we are entering new times, in which the very nature of the human is changing, and it is doing so in a way which both enlightens, and is enlightened by, a range of important work in both 'analytic' and 'continental' philosophy.

So, uh, that's the plan . . .

And so she argued, presenting the work that had been the culmination of the time she had been in New Orleans, bringing together her early work on the early moderns with the feminist theory stuff to present, she thought, a new and exciting theoretical framework. As she watched the people watch fascinated, and then after shower her with praise, she thought back to the tough previous months and felt them decisively behind her, and felt again the joy of creation.

* * *

—Babe it's too much.

—What is?

—This, the waiting, the uncertainty.

—Okay.

—Okay?

—Well, I mean, I can get the money. —I just need time. —I realize that makes you sound like a mobster threatening my knees.

—lol. —Listen, —I have an idea.

—Okay.

—Idea one, you stop saying 'okay'.

—lol, uh, affirmative.

—But idea two . . . —Well, this is kind of maybe crazy.

—I'm listening.

—We interpersonate.

—Okay, well, I was kind of wondering if you were going to suggest that . . .

—And?

There was a pause. In their rooms they each got up and paced a bit, Carrie tense, Jules tense.

—I don't know what I feel about that.

—Okay.

Another pause.

—But convince me.

—Look dude, I'm not going to like beg or anything.

—No, not beg, just convince, show me your perspective?

—Well, I can't just coast like this. It reminds me too much of last time, just being online, talking now and again and then you came here and . . . —I just can't, feels too same and making me miserable. . . . —I need something. . . . —I need some you. . . . —Does not any part of you think it's appealing? To give yourself in that way, to let another see? I do. I know it could be a complete fucking disaster, but so what? . . . —What are we, we're nothing. We try it, it works, we know we gotta do something to bridge the gap. It fails, meh, at least we know. We can't just go on treading water. I can't. Now is the perfect time. I think anyhow. Take a leap. Who knows? What's to lose?

—I see, well, let me think? I can maybe see what you mean.

—Like, this is corny as fuck, but if we can't share the present, we could share our pasts?

—Yeah I see, but like I'm serious about being able to get the money. I can even ask my father . . .

—You don't like the idea.

—No, no, it's just new. I need to think. And it sounds like kind of drastic.

—Maybe you don't feel like I do. Man, I feel it would be a relief! If you don't get that . . .

—I think I do, kinda.

—Obviously I don't want an answer now. Just a suggestion.

—Affirmative.

—Right okay, idea three, you not say 'affirmative' either.

—Fine.

—Oh baby jeebus, we're going to have the same thing again with 'fine' aren't we?

15

All is silence, peace, a house full of appliances softly buzzing or humming, the smell from steak still lingering in the dark (the father's veganism was short-lived), Jules half-snoring from caught nostrils and his larynx.

Then the peace is silently broken.

—Hi, I'm sorry to bother you with this, but something has been on my mind for a while, and I'll get no rest until I get it off my chest. I know that this for you is at least mainly a business and that you don't want to be bothered with customers. But, I'd like you to know that really you've made a very big, good impression on my life and I want to express my gratitude. The fact that you seem to care so much about people inspires me to be better, to try and improve myself. I know this probably sounds silly but it's more than sexual. I can't really say it in words, I just wanted to say thanks.

—Hi I meant, I copied and pasted this!

The day returns, the house's hum outdone by birds outside. Jules wakes, ablutes, opens the window to a cold clear January morning. He presses his tracker and the screen resolves and he sees the chunk of text and worries, chunks of text seldom being good.

But he reads it and realizes that no onerous demand is made, no wanting to meet up or anything like that, and indeed that the message expresses exactly what he did this for, to improve people.

This brings him, though, no relief. He thought this was what he wanted, but now all he feels is sad that he's involved at the heart of the lie that is this man's experience, and sad that people's lives could change by a lie.

He decided, for once and for all, that he had had enough, and he waited a bit before formulating a last message, saying that he was very glad, but that unfortunately he had to stop trading now, for a reason he can't divulge, and then doing so without waiting for a reply.

After he had received Carrie's photo he had more or less stopped his enterprise: he set everything to out of stock, and ceased to log in, and soon things dried up, until the message that had just came. He told the church that sometimes these things just happened, campaigns reach a natural end, but he was glad that they'd at least gotten this far.

Having closed the account, the next day he texted Carrie:

—So look, I'm in for interpersonation.

—For real? I don't think I ever thought you'd actually go for it.

—Well, I want to be with you, and I agree this is a way I can be with you, and can see no other way, so . . .

—Spoken like a true romantic, with premises and conclusion.

—Yeah and anyway, what's the worst that can happen?

—That's the spirit.

—No, I mean, like, it's good. You're right it's a way to try and cross the boundaries. We have a connection. You should take connections where you find them, even if they're odd.

—Oh man, that's *exactly* what I think!

—So like, how does it work? I think I'm ready.

—Oh well, we can't already. You need to dl the app then they need to set it up, so they gotta get all your data. Should take only a couple days. . . . —what changed your mind?

—Nothing really, life is short, fuck it.

— . . . .

—Truly, I mean that in the positivest possible way. It's a gamble, I want to gamble on you.

—That's . . . very, very slightly better

—Sorry. I really am for it. I really want to be with you, that's what I really want.

—Good, me too. Wow. . . . — Man it feels weird, thinking

about it, right?

—It does.

He started typing, deleted, started typing, deleted:

—I've never even close to given so much of myself.

—Me either.

Jules's feelings had followed the same sort of path as Carrie's. Although initially he had contacted her purely because he wanted to set things right, and didn't anticipate or indeed want that anything come of it—he shared her view that it was conceptually bad—nevertheless he felt the same happiness at having her back in his day-to-day and found himself, like her, thinking back to the days and nights they spent together. He had misgivings about the interpersonation thing, but he was nothing if not a gambler, and he thought it worth risking exposing himself if it gave them a way of crossing the boundary imposed by the Atlantic. His currently not-very-satisfactory life would be considerably improved, he thought, if he could share it with her.

But there were limits: he was somewhat confident that even if Carrie wouldn't mind too much about the whole underwear business (she was, after all, very open minded) she certainly would mind, of course, about the fact that he used a naked photo of her. Accordingly, he made sure to delete every trace of his activities from his browsing history, email, and so on, and prepared to make the plunge once his account was ready.

* * *

—Well really, it was really very good.

—Yeah? I kinda hoped so, but it's hard not to think it would be old news.

—No, definitely. I mean, you know, I studied with Butler in NYU, we're still a bit in contact, I bet she'd love to hear about it.

—Oh jeez, wow, I don't know, thank you, that would be amazing, but I think really I'd wanna make sure, like, this is still early work.

—I get it but don't let perfection be the enemy of the good.

—Don't let perfection be the enemy of the good?

—Don't let perfection be the enemy of the good.

Carrie was leaning with her elbow on the bar in a room filled with a couple of patches of students and professors talking. Before her was, as she had quickly googled when she got the chance, a tenured professor of English at a decent university, who was here visiting LSU and had just happened to attend Carrie's talk.

She had been a bit flustered, at first, at the surprise attention, her brain having been ready to shut down after the talk entitled, 'Everything You Wanted To Know About Interpersonation (but were afraid to ask 17th Century British Empiricist John Locke)'. But now she was enjoying it: in the five minutes or so she had already learned a bunch, and even to have this—evidently—respected academic pay attention to her work was a thrill. She got her phone out while the prof ordered them a couple more drinks, to text Jules how it went, in case he happened still to be awake, and saw she'd got a pantact private message from someone who wasn't her friend, and whose name she didn't recognize.

—Hi, sorry if this is rude, I don't want to bother you, it's just you left the site so quickly, I just wanted to make sure everything was okay.

—Is there anything wrong?

—Uh no, anyway, you were saying, uh, what was it, Shelly Turkey?

—Turkel, she's an anthropologist at MIT she's written . . . are you sure you're okay? Sorry.

—No, no nothing, just a random message from a stranger . . . two seconds.

She texted:

—The site?

And continued:

—So this MIT person?

The professor started talking about the way children interact with robots, and Carrie tried to concentrate on her, but she was feeling unsettled. Her phone buzzed:

—Oh sorry! Should have said, it's Derryt from Underthings.

This first confused and then calmed her, and she meant to reply telling him he'd definitely got the wrong person, but was distracted by the professor, and forgot.

The evening passed pleasantly, and a few hours later Carrie and Jordan were heading home.

—So good night?

—*Very* good night. That lady I was talking to, she's friends with Judith Butler, said I could maybe send it to her, like if I write a paper version.

—Wow, that's amazing!

—Yeah man, I'm really happy. It was a nice night. . . . Oh! And some dude sent me a weird message. I forgot about that.

She got out her phone and read it out to Jordan.

—Oh, what did you say?

—Oh nothing, maybe I should tell him he's got the wrong person . . .

She did so:

—Yeah sorry man, you got the wrong person.

—Anyway, yes, good night, did you have a good time?

They were passing through the wasteland behind their apartment, the sound of the crickets buzzing. Carrie, excited, didn't wait for his reply:

—Can't believe how well that talk went. It seemed to be uniformly positive, right?

—Yeah I think so, like I looked around and people seemed like they were really interested. Though I didn't talk to any of the professors afterward, didn't know what to say.

—Ah, you should have, they're kind of cool for academics.

Her phone buzzed.

—Wait, so just to be sure, this isn't you bit.ly/sdgkk?

Confused, Carrie clicked the link, was led to Jules's—or carryon's—page on Underthings, and faced with her Simpsons avatar. Her heart plummeted in her thorax and she reddened. It took her a while to understand what the site was about. She had stopped walking and Jordan, who had first gone ahead, was puzzled.

—What the?

Eventually it became clear: someone, somehow, was pretending to be her.

—Fuck . . . someone's been impersonating me, Jordan.

— . . . ?

—Oh fuck. What the . . . ?

She was thinking of all the awful things that could have been done by her by this pretender.

—Carrie what's wrong?

— . . . .

She was scrolling, not heeding him.

—Carrie?

She raised her head, looked away from the phone, then stared in middle distance, needing to focus all her attention to say some words, her mind overrun and full:

—Somebody has been pretending to be me, I think, on some fetish site.

—What? How do you know?

—Some guy messaged me on pantact, the avatar there is the same as the site, he must have found it . . . who the fuck?

—So somebody is using your photo on a fetish site? Maybe they just, I don't know, found it, could be a weird coincidence.

—Yeah, maybe.

–Like, maybe you don't want to do this . . . this was the guy, the random guy, he told you?

—Yeah.

—You could ask him, what's the deal?

Carrie did, typing:

—I don't know what's going on. That's not me. I have nothing to do with that site . . . how did you even find me?

He quickly replied,

—Sorry, maybe I shouldn't have, should have left you alone, I reverse image searched your avatar when you left the site so suddenly, was just concerned, it seemed sudden. —Wait, so just to be sure, so this isn't you then?

Sending a picture, the naked picture of her Jules had sent him. On eventually realizing what it was, Carrie stopped walking for a bit: Her head and body were full, as her brain tried to work out what she was seeing and why, and her body tried not to lose a grip on itself and scream out or faint. Words were way beyond her.

—You okay? What's wrong, Carrie?

She tried to put the phone down and tried to look into the dark.

—Sorry, you were saying, it was good yeah, your night?

But her voice sort of got caught and choked, and in the dark, its caughtness stood out. He turned to her.

—What is it?

—Nothing . . . I just got sent a nude picture . . . of myself.

— . . . What?

—I mean, from not the person I sent it to . . . fuck, have I been hacked or something?

—Jesus maybe check . . . was this the same guy, again?

She gawped for a moment and said, distracted:

—Yeah, same guy.

—Maybe you have been hacked. And somebody's used your photo. You should check your accounts, if they get one, they can get them all I think.

She didn't even have the space to feel uncomfortable about Jordan's newfound familiarity with the possibilities of hacking.

—Oh fuck-fuck-fuck-fuck. Does it mean I haven't been hacked

if all my apps work?

—I don't know. Log in from the browser.

There was silence for a couple of minutes as she did this, standing among the tall grass, the crickets buzzing, trying to remember passwords in a fuzzy and panicked brain.

—I can . . .

And then she voiced the conclusion that had been in the corner of her mind:

—It must be Jules. Fuck. *He* must have been hacked. Fuck.

She looked at Jordan, her blue eyes now lucid and wide and sober, and asked him, full of question:

—What the fuck?

—You have to contact him.

—He'd never . . . so he must have been hacked. But if he's been hacked, how can I contact him? Fuck! Wait, I have his whatsapp, they wouldn't have hacked his whatsapp? Is that right?

She texted Jules:

—Call me now. I just got a photo of me I sent you. You've been hacked I think.

She moved between concern that Jules had been hacked and the panicked nausea caused by being sent a picture of herself. And said:

—He's probably asleep now.

—Hopefully he's not.

—I can't wait, what, until 3am to find out what the fucking deal is. He must have been hacked . . . he *needs* to sort this, they could have his bank details.

—I hope you see this, please deal now, check all your accounts, someone has hacked your gmail or whatsapp. —HOPE YOU SEE THIS BEFORE MORNING . . . —Someone has been pretending to be me.

Jordan:

—Maybe we should get home?

She didn't listen, just stood there, unable to take her eyes from the notification light on her phone, feeling herself about to burst. Jordan stood in front of her staring at the ground and biting his lip, and he looked so forlorn and worried that the enormity of her situation was made concrete, and he looked up and she looked at him and she made to hug him, and they hugged.

—Hey, what happened?

—Oh, thank god you're up. —I just got a weird message from a guy, from this site Underthings, a picture of me, one I sent you, somebody must have got your details, they're pretending to be me.

There wasn't much of a pause before Jules typed:

—No. —Nobody has my details. It was me. I'm so so so sorry, I had this idea, it doesn't really matter now. But it was me.

—What do you mean it was you?

—I set up the account, I sent the photo. I didn't ever think it would ever come back to you. I quit as soon as we got back, I needed to pretend I was a woman for this website I was making, I'm so sorry.

Carrie:

— . . . .

Jordan said with a strange panic in his voice:

—Carrie what?

Carrie was walking farther back into the wasteland.

—Where are you going?

Jordan watched her recede and then walked-ran after her. Nothing but darkness and crickets, until he saw a light ahead, and followed it. It was her phone lying among long grass. He picked it up, saw the lock screen of a cute dog. The inner pouch where she kept her credit card was empty, and he feared for an irrational second she'd been robbed.

—You dropped your phone!

There was no response but crickets. And from that night on, Carrie was never seen on the Internet again.

Zero Books

CULTURE, SOCIETY & POLITICS

Contemporary culture has eliminated the concept and public figure of the intellectual. A cretinous anti-intellectualism presides, cheer-led by hacks in the pay of multinational corporations who reassure their bored readers that there is no need to rouse themselves from their stupor. Zer0 Books knows that another kind of discourse – intellectual without being academic, popular without being populist – is not only possible: it is already flourishing. Zer0 is convinced that in the unthinking, blandly consensual culture in which we live, critical and engaged theoretical reflection is more important than ever before.

If you have enjoyed this book, why not tell other readers by posting a review on your preferred book site.

Recent bestsellers from Zero Books are:

In the Dust of This Planet

Horror of Philosophy vol. 1

Eugene Thacker

In the first of a series of three books on the Horror of Philosophy, *In the Dust of This Planet* offers the genre of horror as a way of thinking about the unthinkable.

Paperback: 978-1-84694-676-9 ebook: 978-1-78099-010-1

Capitalist Realism

Is there no alternative?

Mark Fisher

An analysis of the ways in which capitalism has presented itself as the only realistic political-economic system.

Paperback: 978-1-84694-317-1 ebook: 978-1-78099-734-6

Rebel Rebel

Chris O'Leary

David Bowie: every single song. Everything you want to know, everything you didn't know.

Paperback: 978-1-78099-244-0 ebook: 978-1-78099-713-1

Cartographies of the Absolute

Alberto Toscano, Jeff Kinkle

An aesthetics of the economy for the twenty-first century.

Paperback: 978-1-78099-275-4 ebook: 978-1-78279-973-3

Malign Velocities

Accelerationism and Capitalism

Benjamin Noys

Long listed for the Bread and Roses Prize 2015, *Malign Velocities* argues against the need for speed, tracking acceleration as the symptom of the ongoing crises of capitalism.

Paperback: 978-1-78279-300-7 ebook: 978-1-78279-299-4

Meat Market

Female Flesh Under Capitalism

Laurie Penny

A feminist dissection of women's bodies as the fleshy fulcrum of capitalist cannibalism, whereby women are both consumers and consumed.

Paperback: 978-1-84694-521-2 ebook: 978-1-84694-782-7

Poor but Sexy

Culture Clashes in Europe East and West

Agata Pyzik

How the East stayed East and the West stayed West.

Paperback: 978-1-78099-394-2 ebook: 978-1-78099-395-9

Romeo and Juliet in Palestine

Teaching Under Occupation

Tom Sperlinger

Life in the West Bank, the nature of pedagogy and the role of a university under occupation.

Paperback: 978-1-78279-637-4 ebook: 978-1-78279-636-7

Sweetening the Pill

or How We Got Hooked on Hormonal Birth Control

Holly Grigg-Spall

Has contraception liberated or oppressed women? *Sweetening the Pill* breaks the silence on the dark side of hormonal contraception.

Paperback: 978-1-78099-607-3 ebook: 978-1-78099-608-0

Why Are We the Good Guys?

Reclaiming your Mind from the Delusions of Propaganda

David Cromwell

A provocative challenge to the standard ideology that Western power is a benevolent force in the world.

Paperback: 978-1-78099-365-2 ebook: 978-1-78099-366-9